The Professionals

Max Hennessy was the pen-name of John Harris. He had a wide variety of jobs from sailor to cartoonist and became a highly inventive, versatile writer. In addition to crime fiction, Hennessy was a master of the war novel and drew heavily on his experiences in both the navy and air force, serving in the Second World War. His novels reflect the reality of war mixed with a heavy dose of conflict and adventure.

Also by Max Hennessy

The RAF Trilogy

The Bright Blue Sky
The Challenging Heights
Once More the Hawks

The Captain Kelly Maguire Trilogy

The Lion at Sea
The Dangerous Years
Back to Battle

The Flying Ace Thrillers

The Mustering of the Hawks
The Mercenaries
The Courtney Entry

The Martin Falconer Thrillers

The Fledglings
The Professionals
The Victors
The Interceptors
The Revolutionaries

The PROFESSIONALS

JOHN HARRIS WRITING AS
MAX HENNESSY

CANELO

First published in the United Kingdom in 1973 by Hutchinson Junior Books

This edition published in the United Kingdom in 2020 by

Canelo
31 Helen Road
Oxford OX2 0DF
United Kingdom

Print ISBN 978 1 80032 717 7
Ebook ISBN 978 1 80032 079 6

Look for more great books at www.canelo.co

Printed and bound in Great Britain by Clays Ltd, Elcograf S.p.A.

Chapter 1

As I had taxied along the line of flares, the cold night air had threatened mist, and the rising moon had not been full enough to pierce it. It had seemed, in fact, almost as if I were lifting the aeroplane off into a blank cloud devoid of horizon or dimensions of any kind, but I had left the ground without thought beyond the feeling of fatalism which, after a year of wartime flying, had become second nature to me.

As the machine rose, however, I saw that it wasn't a thick void of blackness I was flying into but a dim silver-blue landscape cut by the shining ribbon of the Thames estuary to the north. Every roof shone in a pale blue glow and it was possible to pick up railway lines and roads and even, to my surprise, a faint network of hedges. The flares of the aerodrome below looked like a string of glowing beads and I could see more lights on another aerodrome nearer to the edge of London which lay, a dark wartime shadow, sprawled across the winding curves of the river. A searchlight just to the east probed the sky with an uncertain pencil of white.

I felt I could have sailed on for ever to the moon and for once the old irritated feeling of frustration which had been growing on me for weeks fell away. 'Just the old war horse sniffing for the smell of battle,' Sykes had once called it and he was probably right.

Sykes, too, was somewhere out there beyond the wing tip in this silver-grey brilliance, and once, over the rippling fabric of the wing I even thought I saw him. I don't suppose I did but the thought that I might have done destroyed the feeling of loneliness. There were three other young men out there with us, too – Williamson, Graves and McSpadden, none of them much older than I was, all as anxious, probably *more* anxious because they were all inexperienced and hadn't properly finished their training. But, with the outcry that was going up from Parliament that London was being bombed and homes were in danger, they'd been pushed into the air with Sykes and myself who not long before had been instructing them in the arts of advanced flying.

Personally I thought the panic a lot of nonsense, but London in 1916 had got itself into a state, and *John Bull*, a rampant, rubbishy magazine if ever there was one, and a few Members of Parliament, anxious to show the population that they had their safety at heart, had kicked up such a fuss there was even talk of bringing back a squadron or two from France. Considering how many men were being killed every week over there and considering that nobody had turned a hair at the awful slaughter on the Somme, it seemed to me they were showing more concern for their own careers than they were for the course of the war.

But London was a strange place those days. It had never once seemed like home since I'd returned and its people were curiously more foreign than the peasants in France. Home for me had become a group of Bessoneau hangars and shabby wooden huts with oiled silk windows on a bleak windswept field near the Belgian border, and a line of lattice-tailed FE2bs or DH1s or the spidery shapes of BEs among the mist. After two years of war London was full of Australians, New Zealanders, Indians, Canadians, Belgians in tall forage caps and Russians in dark blue, and even odd nationalities like Serbs, Montenegrins and Portuguese. The civilians seemed unconcerned with the war and only busy with their own affairs, rationing, making money and keeping cheerful despite the losses in

France. They were far more occupied with the Zeppelins than they need have been – because they didn't seem to cause much inconvenience apart from a few bangs in the night – and their attitude to the war was nauseating. In France in 1916, you never heard much about patriotism and the sort of 'Scrag the Hun' talk that the sporting parsons in England liked to offer. After eighteen months in uniform, I had found my own attitude had become a sort of sheepish cynicism at having let myself be deluded into thinking it was a romantic adventure and rushing into it headlong when so many others had stayed at home. It was a strange attitude for someone not yet nineteen but there was never the same hilarious keenness for battle in France that there was in London, and never the same outcry when a night's sleep was disturbed.

I wrenched my attention back to the job in hand. I wasn't floating about in the night sky above London to muse on what was wrong with the war. I was there to stop the Zeppelins and it was something you couldn't do if you didn't concentrate.

Below me, occasionally, I saw a pinpoint of light which indicated that life still went on down there in the dark, even once the silver trail of smoke from a moving train. I peered at the instruments but it was impossible to make them out and the only thing I was aware of was a length of worsted attached to the centre section strut which flicked back at me in the slipstream. I had made it just long enough to tickle my forehead above the windscreen so I could feel it in the dark. If I ceased to feel it I would know I was in a side slip, and I was at 10,000 feet because that was the ceiling of the machine I was flying and I knew I'd reached it by the sloppy feel of the controls.

Their lack of grip seemed to be reflected in my life. The Battle of the Somme was over now, with God alone knew how many dead on either side and nothing accomplished, and there was a sort of desperation in the air, and when they had sent me back to England and Home Establishment I had already become sick of the war. I had rushed off in 1915 straight from school – indeed I'd still really been a scholar, jealous of my elder brother Geoffrey, who'd been wounded in the trenches, and itching to show him I could be as able in battle as he was. Perhaps he was the lucky one. He had died in a flying accident the year before, still – like all his generation – full of the hopes of victory. Like the rest of us, he'd been waiting for the first sign of a crack in the German line – that fortress of trenches that ran from Switzerland to the sea – and he had died never knowing that the battle of the new Kitchener Armies, which had been expected to shatter it, had ended with no more than a mere dent. Those of us who had survived the ordeal had lost something in the making of that dent.

I was numb with the cold. We had been waiting for months now and no one had ever seen a Zeppelin, though occasionally we'd seen the bright splashes of their bombs below. The draught was inching its way down my neck and I pulled my scarf tighter. It had a faint perfume about it that reminded me of Jane, who'd knitted it for me. I'd known Jane Widdows all my life and if my brother had lived our families would have been joined by marriage because he had been engaged to her sister.

I shifted in the cockpit, trying to catch some of the warm air from the engine. There seemed to be more cloud about now, heavy and edged with silver and I could see it closing in fast. I hoped it would let me get down first and I wondered where Sykes was. He hadn't changed much since I'd first met him in France the previous year. Spare and languid, he still favoured the stock, immaculate breeches and whip of the cavalry.

'Ought to wear spurs,' I teased him.

'Not really.' He was always so bland you never knew whether he was serious or not. 'Tear the fabric gettin' in and out.' He had graduated to flying, like so many others of his breed, when machine guns and trenches had put a stop to horses.

Doubtless, at that moment he was blinking round him at the sky, as though wondering why he was there at all, and looking as if he were bewildered to find himself skilful enough to fly an aeroplane at all. In fact, he was a good pilot and was made of whipcord and steel springs, and his attitude of airy indifference was only because, without charging horses and lances and sabres, the war had become an unholy chore for him. Only the discovery of the Flying Corps had stopped him dying of sheer boredom, and now, wry-necked from an old wound, handsome, hiding his true professionalism under a cloak of rank amateurism, like me he was itching to get back to France.

I was frozen stiff by this time, despite the two jerseys I wore, the leather coat, the silk and woollen gloves under the leather gauntlets, the heavy knee boots and the woollen balaclava under my flying helmet, to say nothing of the seven-foot long khaki scarf Jane had given me which wound round my neck about three times before it tucked into my jacket. A drip of condensation off the centre section hit me in the face with a hard slap and brought me back to the present and I stared round me, searching again. The machine was vaguely outlined by the blue-yellow flames of the exhaust but they weren't enough to help in seeing the instruments, and I turned on to a new course, heading south by guesswork. The engine was giving full revs but it sounded as though it was about to fall apart. The BE12 had always had that effect on me. The big four-bladed propeller seemed to increase the vibration of the engine and I liked the machine as much as I'd liked its predecessor, the BE2C. That had been a sick joke and the BE12 wasn't much better. It was really nothing more than a higher-powered single-seater BE2C, armed with a forward-firing Vickers gun. The front seat had been taken out to make room for a new 140 h.p. engine which looked enormous, and the machine had a look of power. But we all knew it was a wash-out, slow and lacking in manoeuvrability, and we all guessed its days were already numbered. Only the fact that the Zeppelins it was being used to hunt were slower still gave it any value at all.

There was a front moving up and the clouds seemed to be building up fast now. I went through a group of them blind, watching the mist snatched past the wings, and as I emerged and swung back on course I suddenly found to my horror that I was thundering down on the side of a cliff emerging from another layer of cloud just ahead. My hair stood on end and in the fraction of a second before I did anything about it I found myself wondering where I was, because no cliffs I knew reached as high as 10,000 feet.

It was only after a spasm of sheer terror that I realized that the 'cliff' was moving, too, and I almost jumped out of the cockpit. It was no cliff I was staring at! It was the Zeppelin I was supposed to be chasing!

I gaped at the huge shape, startled. It couldn't be! After weeks of searching, surely I hadn't found one! For a moment, I couldn't believe my eyes and had to blink to realize I wasn't seeing things, then I got hold of myself and began to concentrate as I closed in for a better look at it. It seemed half a mile long and I had to turn my head from one side to the other to take in the whole leviathan shape of it. I knew they were in the region of 500 feet long but I had never dreamed they would look as big as this one looked.

Two or three small cars hung underneath, glistening in the moonlight, and I could see cabin lights. The rubberized covering of the vast machine was daubed a sort of grey-yellow and even as I watched, wondering how anything as big as an ocean liner could remain suspended in the air, I saw a black Maltese cross float past in front of me and the letters LZ and a number that didn't even register, and I came to life with a jerk.

I was here to destroy this gigantic thing not look at it! My gun contained the new Brock and Pomeroy incendiary bullets and all I had to do was fire! I gulped, feeling dwarfed by the colossal size of the monster, and reached out to cock the gun. The 'clack' seemed as loud over the roar of the engine as a revolver shot.

The vast gasbag was slipping past me now at what seemed a tremendous speed and I swung the BE round, cursing its poor performance and thumping on the cockpit surround in a fury of frustration. Gradually the Zeppelin swam into view once more, like some huge whale gliding effortlessly through the air, and as it came into my sights again, I reached for the trigger and was just about to press it when the whole sky lit up as both the Zeppelin and BE were caught in the cone of three searchlights at once. For a moment, I was dazzled, and every spar and strut and ripple of fabric on the BE was picked out in a hard blue-white light. I could even see the stitches alongside the cockpit and the threads of the turnbuckles on the bracing wires. The Zeppelin was below me now, a vast black cigar, illumined along its edges by the searchlights' beams and it looked so big I felt I could easily have landed on top of it, running my wheels along the smooth surface and coming to stop without trouble before I fell off at the other end.

I pushed the nose down, certain I had it at my mercy, and fired. Almost at once, I heard bullets singing past me and one of them hit the exhaust stack with a *whangg* that made me almost jump out of my seat and I realized that hidden somewhere along its huge envelope this giant had a sting.

Swinging away instinctively, I pulled the machine round as fast as I could and gave it every ounce of power it had. I caught the glow of exhausts from the Maybach engines that drove the Zeppelin along, then, as the searchlights caught me in the over-spill of light, the German gunners snapped off a few more shots. My heart was thumping in my chest. The Zeppelin was so big I couldn't possibly miss if I could just get in close enough, and the Brock and Pomeroy bullets would do the rest.

A Zeppelin had been shot down over London not long before by a man called Leefe-Robinson of 39 Squadron, flying a machine exactly like the one I was in. I'd been told about it. He'd seen the whole rear part of the great torpedo-shaped thing glow as he'd fired then there had been the thump of exploding gas, and the giant had dropped out of the sky shedding chunks of framework, pieces of molten metal and blazing fragments of fabric. It had fallen at Cuffley, in Middlesex, in a vast flare of flame. As I stared at the airship moving in front of me I had a momentary vision of myself getting the Victoria Cross as Leefe-Robinson had done, going home to Jane a hero, and lording it over Sykes for a change instead of him lording it over me; then I was dragging that ugly lumbering aeroplane round again, wildly excited and scared stiff of losing that gigantic enemy machine ahead of me in the dark. I was coming up to it again now and the searchlights had picked it up once more. It was mine, I thought – I couldn't miss – and I felt sick with excitement and triumph. Then, as I reached for the trigger of the gun, the searchlights switched off again, either because they'd seen me or because they'd lost the Zeppelin and as I swung round to come up underneath the monster, in the fraction of a second when I tried to get my eyes used to the dark again after the glare, directly in front of me I caught a glimpse of square black wings silhouetted against the line of lights on one of the cabins of the Zeppelin, and heavy struts and two vast exhaust stacks.

I had found Sykes.

–

I wrenched at the stick and kicked the rudder bar and, as the BE slid round in a skidding turn it was never built for, I shoved the nose down so that all the dust in the bottom of the cockpit seemed to come up at me and fill my nostrils. Small fragments of grit hit me in the face and for a moment I felt sure I'd pulled the wings off, then I was staring into nothingness again and there was no sign of Sykes and no sign of the Zeppelins. As I found it once more – up above me – I saw what looked like a rain storm glistening in the moonlight below it as the vast shape lifted over my head like an elevator and disappeared into the cloud.

The commander of the Zeppelin, startled by the shooting, had jettisoned his water ballast to lift the airship two or three hundred feet in a matter of seconds, and I jammed the throttle forward and pulled the stick back to climb after him. But that cow of a BE12 had done all it was ever likely to do. It had never been built for air fighting and there was nothing left in it and I felt the stick go sloppy again. The nose dropped and I had to push the stick forward to prevent her stalling, and as I did so somewhere a mile or so away I caught a brief glimpse of moonlight on a wing surface and as the cloud closed again and the glint disappeared, I guessed it was Sykes and bitterly hoped he'd been as terrified as I was.

My heart was still thumping but there was nothing I could do now except sit and watch that vast monster emerge from the clouds again and glide out to sea above me untouched. It only served to make me feel more savage than ever.

Angry with myself, angry with Sykes, angry even with the Zeppelin commander, I began to concentrate on getting myself down safely. The clouds had closed completely now and the darkness seemed like the inside of a cow. 'This is the trick of the thing,' Sykes had once said in that cheerful inconsequential way of his. 'Any fool can get an aeroplane off the ground. It's a different matter putting it down again.'

There was a story that not long before a man in a neighbouring squadron had slammed his machine down so hard in the dark on to the unseen earth he had driven the struts of his undercarriage up into the fuselage and, since he had also broken every blade of his propeller clean off at the same time, he had failed to notice what had happened. He had switched off the engine at once and thankfully jumped down to *terra firma* – and nearly broke his back because it was only a couple of feet below him in the blackness. It was probably an apocryphal story but it showed it paid to be careful and, because I couldn't see the altimeter unwinding, I kept the end of the worsted just in front of my nose, guessing the speed by the sound of the wind in the wires.

I found the line of flares eventually and carefully kept them in sight, lowering myself in gentle S-turns until I could see mechanics standing in the glow of the flames. At 500 feet I fired a Very light and the red ball curled away dazzling me momentarily. An answering flare came up from the ground and I was as tense as a cat after a mouse as I concentrated every faculty I had into putting the machine down without breaking my neck. Night landings were still new enough to be frightening and there were patches of ground mist about still, blurring the view, so I kept close to the flares for safety, kicking the rudder to bring me nearer. The first of the fires flashed past, then I saw drifting smoke and a couple of faces lit by the glow, and holding the stick back, I let the machine sink slowly to the earth until both wheels and tail touched together and the rumble beneath me told me I was down.

–

Sykes was standing inside the mess hut, unwinding a scarf about forty feet long from round his neck. There was black on his cheeks and his eyes looked like saucers where his goggles had protected them from the cordite as he'd fired his gun. He struggled out of a leather coat and dropped it on the floor, and one of the mess staff immediately picked it up. Sykes thanked him with a condescending grace that wasn't a bit offensive but when I dropped mine I noticed no one rushed to help *me*.

It was typical of Sykes. His background was Eton, fox-hunting and cavalry, and his manner was the well-bred politeness of generations of wealth. He had a string of initials a yard long – C. L. W. B. D. Sykes – but no one ever called him anything else but 'Bill' because the only character with that name that most people knew was the one in Dickens. It certainly didn't suit him. It was short and blunt and ugly while Sykes was slender and handsome, despite his wry neck, and full of the sort of lazy charm that made lesser mortals like me melt in front of him.

He stared up at the sky as though trying to assess just what was happening in the darkness, vague and faintly weary. 'Bit tricky up there for a minute, young Falconer,' he observed.

'You saw me?' I said.

'Couldn't miss you.' He gave a faint smile. 'Rushin' in! Angels fear to tread and all that. Have to be more careful, old boy. Dangerous, that sort of thing, shouldn't wonder.'

His casualness infuriated me. '*I'll* have to be careful!' I snorted. 'You came right across ahead of me.'

He blinked. 'After the sausage,' he said. 'Fearfully excited.'

'What the hell were you doing there anyway?'

'Chasing the old Zepp, like you. Hadn't the foggiest where I was. Had you?'

I stared at him. He gazed at me, his head on one side because of the wound he'd got in France the previous year and looking like an amiable setter. I grinned, completely disarmed.

'No,' I said.

He beamed, as though it were the most important thing in the world that we shouldn't lose our tempers with each other.

'Get shot at?' he asked.

'Couple of times. How about you?'

'Same with knobs on. Feller on top with a gun. Quite bad-tempered. Got a few holes through my centre section. Hit you at all?'

'One on the exhaust. Thought it had fallen off.'

'Might well have – from a BE.' He smiled again. 'Ought to do this sort of thing more cunningly, y'know. Come in from opposite sides at the same time. Like we planned in France for tackling two-seaters. Can't shoot at both of us at once.'

'Only one problem,' I said.

'What's that?'

'What do we do when we meet in the middle in the dark?'

He chuckled. 'Same as tonight,' he said. 'Take violent evasive action.'

'This ripping off the wings, and plummeting to earth like a spent rocket in a death dive.'

He blinked, then he grinned. 'Been reading too much *John Bull*,' he observed.

I glanced at the sky. 'Actually,' I said, 'I don't much enjoy being an intrepid birdman in the dark, do you? I reckon they should at least fit us up with lighted instruments. Or a pair of Mark I Owl's Eyes.'

A sergeant put his head in the door. 'The others are coming in now, sir,' he called.

We went to the door to see what sort of mess the others would make of their landings and stood outside the hut, staring into the blackness. The flares were still burning and you could see the smoke from them, illuminated by their own flames, drifting away in long yellow curves down the line. Somewhere up above I could hear a big 140-horse engine roaring. It was over to the east of the field by the end of the landing area and it sounded strange.

Then it dawned on me I could hear not one but two. As I listened, the noise died away until there was only a subdued muttering in the darkness.

'There are two of 'em out there,' I said. 'And they're *both* coming in!'

'That ought to be jolly,' Sykes observed flatly, his breath hanging in clouds on the chilly night air. 'Especially if they come in together.'

As he spoke, I saw the red ball of a Very light drop out of the sky. 'There's one of 'em!'

Another red ball came down at roughly the same level as the first but to the port side of the landing area and almost at the same time a third red ball curved up from the ground. It was in answer to the first machine that was drifting in on its final descent from the starboard side of the runway, but I heard two engines roar and I guessed that the pilot of the second machine, which was coming in from the port side, had probably not seen the first machine's signal because of his own wings and had assumed that the answering red ball was for him.

Sykes stared at me. 'For God's sake,' he said sharply and started to run.

I was heading for the officer in charge of the flarepath to warn him but he had anticipated me and I saw a couple of flares rise into the darkness. We were all too late. I heard a motor scream agonisedly somewhere just above me, as the panic-stricken pilot did just what I'd done when I'd seen Sykes and shoved the throttle forward in an attempt to dodge, then there was a soft crunching noise above it, and an aeroplane whirred past out of the darkness, a great black shape of square wings and struts.

It seemed to be moving crabwise and, as it was silhouetted for a moment by the glow of the flames, I saw its wingtip had collapsed and the aileron was clattering wildly. The next moment, it had thumped into the ground and I saw fragments fly off as it slithered along the grass, churning up the turf, then it came to a stop, tilted up on its nose and dropped back on to its tail, still rocking slightly. I reached it almost as it stopped. The pilot was head down in the cockpit, snoring loudly through the blood that came from his nose, and I snatched at his safety belts and began to drag him from the cockpit. I could smell petrol and firmly expected the machine to go up in flames.

Somewhere behind me I heard a low 'thud' and saw the cockpit glow, then a couple of mechanics arrived and we heaved the pilot out and dragged him away from the machine with trailing feet, still blowing blood from a pulped nose. It was Williamson, and as far as I could see he was all right except for a broken nose and the loss of a few teeth. He'd mend, I decided, and as I let him sink to the dew-laden grass, I turned round, wondering what had happened to the other machine.

It was at the far end of the runway, burning fiercely, and I caught glimpses of dark figures hovering round it, then the blood wagon bounced past me over the turf, its red cross picked out by the blaze, the Major clinging to the running board and shouting at the driver.

–

The smell of oily smoke still filled the mess hut as Sykes thrust a glass in my hand. 'Drink that up,' he said.

I swallowed it without a word. When I'd donned uniform I'd been a non-drinker and a non-smoker, but eighteen months of war had changed all that and I swallowed it without turning a hair.

As Sykes sat down, the Major came in. He was a nutty little man with a leathery face and a limp that was a relic of an old crash.

'Anything been heard of McSpadden, sir?' Sykes asked.

The Major shook his head and asked for a drink. As he turned he looked old and tired. 'Three,' he said bitterly. 'I expect he's in the sea.'

'Two, sir,' I pointed out. 'Williamson'll be all right.'

'Not for a month or two,' he said. 'Call it three.'

He swallowed his drink and vanished. I glanced across at Sykes, who was sprawled in a cane chair by the bar. My coat was still on the floor where I'd dropped it and we were both grimy with the oil from our engines and the cordite from our guns after our scuffle in the night sky. Huddled in his stained jacket, his hair flat and spiky where he'd wrenched off his flying helmet and goggles, Sykes suddenly looked weary.

'What a perfectly bloodstained night,' he said slowly. 'One dead, one in the sea, one injured. It seems to me there needs to be a little organization brought into this night-flying lark.'

For a moment I said nothing. Ideas had been burning in my mind ever since I'd watched the ambulance crash past to pick up what was left of Graves. 'We ought to be at different heights,' I said.

Sykes lifted his head slowly. His eyes were a brilliant blue and they seemed to glow in the light of the lantern on the bar. I tried to explain.

'We ought to be at different heights,' I said again. 'And flying different courses so we can't meet. It's too slapdash this way.'

He managed to look interested, but it seemed an effort. 'What do you suggest?'

'Well,' I said, 'it seems a bit futile to let a dozen machines in the air at once when they can't see each other. There ought to be a system of patrols.'

Sykes gestured. 'Go on, Brat,' he said. 'For a schoolboy, you talk a lot of sense.'

I leaned on the bar. 'Suppose machines were sent up to patrol at eight, nine and ten thousand feet,' I said. 'Each pilot with a beat, and orders – strict orders – not to leave it in case he collides with someone else. He stays up there, patrolling up and down for two hours, keeping a sharp look out, and only moves off it if he sees the Hun. When his time's up he comes down, at – say – the north end of his beat, by which time another machine is relieving him at the south end. This way no two machines are in the same spot at once or coming in at the same time. That way we ought to cover a lot of ground without any of the trouble we've had tonight.'

Sykes smiled and rubbed his nose. It was well-shaped but large and bony. 'Makes sense,' he observed. 'Ought to go a long way if you survive. I'll put your ideas to the Old Man. He'll probably put you up for a general.'

Chapter 2

The clouds that had enabled the Zeppelin to escape from us closed in fast. The wind coming out of the north-west was full of rain and there were great pools of water along the folds of the flying field. The Bessoneaux flapped wanly in the wind and the mechanics went about their business with their heads down inside their coat collars, their noses raw and red-looking.

'Week-end leave seems to be indicated,' Sykes said.

We got the tender to take us to the station and in London I grabbed the first taxi I saw and shouted 'Liverpool Street' at the driver.

'Here, hang on!' Sykes was just behind me, pushing his bag in alongside me. 'I'm coming too.'

'Where to?'

'Liverpool Street.'

'Do you live my way?'

'I dunno. Where do *you* live?'

We stared at each other. I'd known him for several months, first in France and now again back in England, and it had never occurred to either of us to find out where the other came from.

'Fynling,' I said. 'East of Norwich.'

He grinned. 'Hathersett,' he said. 'Bit to the west.'

I stared at him. 'Well, I'm blowed!' I said. 'How long have you lived there?'

He blinked. 'All my life,' he said. 'How about you?'

'Six or seven years.'

He smiled. 'Almost neighbours. Nice place, Fynling. Met a cracking girl down that way when I was convalescent after being wounded.'

'We ought to get together some time,' I said. 'Do you shoot?'

'Not as well as you.'

I grinned, enjoying the thought of being able to show the great Sykes something. 'I can get a gun and a punt,' I said. 'I'll give you a few tips.'

He looked interested. 'Can you get away with it?'

'We're not supposed to with the war on but I know the local bobby. He always looks the other way. I go out occasionally. You should try it.'

'Too busy,' he said. 'Horses are *my* downfall.'

We picked up the Norwich train and sat beaming at each other. There was a little man in the compartment who looked like a London businessman going home for the week-end and he got into conversation.

'What happened to the Big Push?' he asked.

'What Big Push?' Sykes stared at him with that blank look he always put on for people he disliked. It made him look stupid.

The little man frowned. 'The one on the Somme,' he said. 'Someone made a mess of it, didn't they?'

'Germans.' Sykes nodded knowingly. 'Didn't play fair.'

The little man stared at him. '*Didn't play fair!*' he said. 'It's not a game out there, you know.'

Sykes, his head still askew from an old painful wound, stared at him. 'It *isn't*?' he said, feigning amazement.

'They'll have to start another one now.' The little man's indignation was immense. 'Another push, I mean.'

'Oh, they will,' Sykes agreed. 'As soon as the dust settles from this one.'

'What's it going to be like?'

'What?'

'When they start a new push.'

Sykes shrugged. 'Pushier than this one, I expect.'

The little man refused to let us alone and we were glad when he got out at Colchester. As we left on the last leg, we saw an aeroplane moving along with the train. 'Avro,' Sykes said, studying it. 'Nice buses. Steady as a rock. Once heard of one that took off on its own and was chased by the pilot in a car for fifty miles. He caught it up just as it landed. Put itself down like a feather.'

'Bit too steady for me,' I said.

He stared at me. 'That's a funny thing to say,' he observed. 'Bit too steady? Always thought that was the one thing we were after in aeroplanes.'

I shrugged. 'It seems to me,' I said, 'that if an aeroplane's nice and steady to shoot *from*, it's going to be nice and steady to shoot *at*. The sort of aeroplane I'm looking for is one that isn't nice and steady, and if you move the joystick it'll flick over on to its back in a second. If it'll do that it'll probably be hard to hit.'

He looked thoughtful. 'You know,' he said. 'You're a studious old buster, all things considered.

Only chap I ever came across who *thought* about flying. You've got quite a point there.'

As we parted on the platform at Norwich, he waved. 'Have to try to get together,' he said. 'I sometimes get over to Fynling. How're you getting home?'

'Train,' I said. 'How about you?'

'I expect someone will have sent the motor to meet me.'

'Oh!' I decided Sykes' family must be important if they could afford a motor car.

'Awful fag,' he said. 'Keeps stopping.'

I hadn't told anyone I was coming home so there was no one to meet me at Fynling. But the grocer's shop was just down the road and I could see the horse and trap outside. I put my head through the door.

'Going my way?' I asked.

The grocer grinned. 'Hello, Master Martin,' he said. 'Yes, we are. This very minute. Jump in.'

He dropped me on the main road outside the village. It was all achingly familiar – a watery sun and the usual cold wind coming from the east, and marshes stretching as far as the eye could travel to the North Sea. It was already all so much a part of me, I couldn't ever imagine not wanting to come home. It was here I'd learned to sail and here I'd first used a gun.

There was no one at home when I arrived. My mother was involved with hospital work, while my father was lecturing for the army at one of the colleges in Cambridge. The cook greeted me as if I were her own long-lost son, however, and enfolded me to her vast bosom until I was breathless.

'How about a bit of grub, Cookie?' I said as she released me.

'Just you sit down there, Master Martin,' she said, shoving things aside on the kitchen table, 'and I'll have it ready in a jiffy. It'll have to be bacon and eggs, though, because it's hard to get much else these days.'

'Sounds fine,' I said.

'How many eggs?'

'Make it a round dozen,' I suggested, and she slapped at me with the tea-towel.

When I'd eaten I went to my room to change into civvies. It was full of the model aeroplanes I'd made while at school. They looked extraordinarily flimsy now and I realized how flying had changed since the war – how *I'd* changed. Suddenly I was aware of a tremendous feeling of frustration and had to get out of the house. Like so many more I was divorced by a whole age from the period before the war had started, different from those who were too young to know it and a complete alien to those who were old enough to have had a life before it. Suddenly flattened, I went outside and dug out a bicycle from the woodshed to ride over to Jane's. The Widdowses had farmed the land around for generations and I'd spent half my life in and out of their house, helping with the harvest, rabbiting, shooting – even labouring while I was waiting to go into uniform.

Mr Widdows was in the stackyard with an old man and a boy too young to be in the army, dragging things about that were far too heavy for a man of his age.

'Hello, Martin,' he said, clearly glad to take a breather.

'Where's Jane?'

He paused, glanced sideways at the old man and blew his nose heavily; it seemed he was taking time to think – almost as though he needed to choose his words. It had an odd, isolating effect because I'd always regarded their family almost as my own, sharing their sorrows and secrets and joys, so that it was curiously hurtful to feel he had to think before he spoke.

'She's out,' he said.

'Norwich? Shopping?'

'Think so. I don't really know.'

'When will she be back?'

'Don't know that either. Don't really know what she gets up to at all these days. She got a job working with a typewriting machine in Norwich, y'know. Released some chap for the army. Seems to like it.'

The world had changed, I decided. I couldn't ever remember a time when I'd come home and Jane hadn't been around to torment me.

'How's Edith?' I asked.

Sometimes I felt that Edith belonged to a different world now. She'd married a doctor from Norwich after my brother had been killed.

He grinned. 'Expecting,' he said.

'Oh? I'm glad.'

'Her husband's in France now. Base hospital. At least he ought to be safe there unless one of these damned Zeppelins drops a bomb. Nasty things, Zeppelins.'

'Yes, I know,' I said. 'One shot at me the other night. Hit me too. Or at least, my machine.'

'It did? Are *you* up there after them?'

'When we get a chance.'

'They're making a mess of London, I hear.'

'Not so I've noticed,' I said. 'It looked all right as I passed through.'

It was his turn to look surprised. 'I thought they were,' he said.

'Newspaper talk.'

'They killed thirteen people in King's Lynn last year.'

I shrugged. It showed the gulf that existed between us these days. I felt like saying 'They killed thousands and thousands on the Somme,' but I didn't. It wouldn't have been fair, and I noticed he looked older and more tired these days. Since the war, the days of being a gentleman farmer were over. He had to do the work himself now that his manager and his men had disappeared into the army.

'The German High Seas Fleet bombarded Lowestoft,' he went on. 'Some time back. Did you hear? Knocked down a few houses on the front, and hit the pier and a convalescent home. Two men, and a woman and a child killed. One shell landed in Oulton Broad two miles away.'

He also seemed to sense that we were different and was trying to reach me by giving me an account of *his* war. His was a trivial affair, though, and he knew it, but it gave him a sense of belonging to the vast tragedy that was taking place in France.

There seemed to be no point in hanging around so I rode slowly home via the village in the hope of seeing someone I knew. Leave was always a bit of an anticlimax because everybody of my own age was in one of the services or working.

As I passed the station, I noticed the signal was down and heard the thin whistle of a train approaching. I glanced at the clock and saw it was the afternoon slow in from Norwich and wondered if Jane was on it. I decided to wait and went into the village shop to buy a newspaper.

'Hello, Master Martin,' the old woman behind the counter said. 'Back on leave again?'

I didn't know where she got the 'again' from. I wasn't home all *that* often.

'Yes,' I said. 'Home again.'

'Shooting at them Zeppelins?'

'Trying to.'

It was the usual cheerful meaningless banter that went on between all those at home and all those who came from France. For the most part, though, it was harmless and no one took offence at it.

I glanced at the newspaper in the doorway while I waited for the train to arrive. It contained the usual rubbish hailing the Somme as a major break-through, and there was no mention of the enormous numbers of casualties, only a lot about what had been achieved. It listed the villages which had been captured and enumerated the prisoners, but it didn't mention that the villages were only a mile or two beyond the line. Considering the lives lost, they seemed a pretty poor return, and I decided that the newspapers knew nothing at all of what was happening and were making up a lot of what they printed.

As I came out of the shop, a woman I didn't know stopped me. I'd never seen her before, though her face seemed vaguely familiar, and I guessed she was one of the wealthy people from London who'd hurriedly bought houses in the area to get away from the strict rationing of the city to a place where they could buy country eggs, milk and butter, and where they were safe from the Zeppelins. She was a large woman with pince-nez spectacles and a hat with a feather in it that might have looked fine in Bloomsbury but looked as much in place in the middle of Fynling as a cow with a wooden leg.

'Young man!' she said.

I looked up from the newspaper.

'I haven't seen you around here before,' she said.

'I haven't been around here,' I said as politely as I could. 'At least not for a while.'

'My nephew,' she went on loudly, 'is in the army.'

Obviously, I thought, her nephew was as stupid as I was.

'On the staff of General Horne.'

Clearly he wasn't *that* stupid but I couldn't imagine what business of mine it was.

'He's only twenty-three,' she went on 'and he's a captain,' and I decided her nephew was luckier than most and wondered who'd pulled the strings for him.

'How old are *you*?' she asked.

Again I couldn't imagine what business of hers it was but I was still caught a little unawares and I told her.

'Going on for nineteen,' I said, stretching it a little.

'You're not in uniform.'

'No.' I was just going to tell her why when she pressed on, ploughing over me like a ship in full sail.

'I also have a nephew of twenty-two,' she said. 'He has joined the Flying Corps. Most young men of nearly nineteen are in the Services.'

It suddenly dawned on me what she was getting at. She was the sort of woman who talked glibly of 'the field of honour' and 'our noble allies' and 'We will not tolerate the cry of "Peace" until the Hun has been put where he belongs', the sort of childless woman who could happily write to the newspapers to tell other women how to lose an only son without too much heart-searching, and liked to think of British soldiers chasing the Germans round their trenches with the cheerful glint of battle in their eyes as if they were ratting in an allotment. It made me squirm.

I was just going to tell her exactly what I was doing there when she thrust an envelope in my hand.

'It's quite obvious,' she said, 'you are a great deal in need of encouragement.'

As she swept away, I stared down at the envelope and as I opened it I saw it contained a white feather.

I felt my face going red and the fury boiling up inside, but she had disappeared now into a shop further down the street and I stood holding the envelope, wondering whether I had the courage to go after her and throw it in her stupid face.

I was still staring at it when I heard Jane's voice. The train had arrived while I'd been talking and she was running across the road towards me from the station. I turned and she flung her arms round me and hugged me as I swung her off her feet.

'You didn't say you were coming home!' she said excitedly, her eyes shining.

'I didn't know,' I grinned. 'I just managed to snatch a week-end.'

'It's lovely to see you. What's the matter though? You were looking as though you were wanting to murder someone.'

The smile died. 'I was,' I said. I opened my hand and showed her the white feather. 'I've just had that given to me.'

'*You?*' She stared, her face growing angry. 'But who...?' She stopped. 'Oh, no, don't say that stupid woman's been at it again.'

'What stupid woman?'

'Catlow-Hope's her name. Gosh, she's a bit out of date, isn't she? That sort of thing stopped when conscription came in. Her husband's some sort of importer in London. They've taken a house here and she's been making a nuisance of herself all round the district.' She began to giggle. 'Fancy, though! *You!* Of all people!'

It didn't seem all that funny to me, but her laughter was infectious, and I laughed with her.

'She always picks the wrong men,' she giggled. '*Always.*'

'She told me her nephew was on the staff of General Horne.'

'I'm not surprised. He's an awful little toad. They all are. She's got several and they're all as bad.' She frowned. 'I'll see that she learns who you are.'

'Oh, blow the white feather!' I said. 'It's not that important. It's much better to talk about you. What are we going to do for the week-end?'

She frowned. It was her father all over again and it was so unexpected it was like a smack in the face. She recovered quickly, however. 'It's too late in the year to sail,' she said. 'It's freezing. We can always walk, though.'

I didn't push the matter but I wondered why for the first time she wasn't eager to spend her time with me. 'How're you getting home?' I asked.

'Walking.'

'I've got a bike here. You can get on the cross-bar if you like. You've done it before.'

'I was less well padded behind then, too.' She smiled and as I brought the bicycle across she lifted herself on.

We talked as I pedalled and I asked her how her job was going.

'Oh, all right.' She didn't seem too sure. 'Helping a solicitor doesn't seem a very positive way of pushing the war along.'

'I should forget the war if I were you,' I suggested. 'Just be around to look spiffing when warriors like me come home. That's the best war effort I can think of.'

She was silent for a moment, clutching her parcels and balancing on the cross-bar, and I saw she was frowning.

'What's wrong?' I asked. 'You've gone quiet.'

She laughed but it sounded a little forced to me. 'It's the war, perhaps,' she said. 'It gives you the pip occasionally. Everybody disappearing and all that.'

After a couple of miles I came to the conclusion she was heavier than I'd thought and decided I needed a rest, and we stopped on a stone bridge across one of the dykes and sat on the parapet. I took out a packet of cigarettes without thinking and offered her one. She took it and I lit my own and offered the light to her. Then it dawned on me what she'd done.

'What's the matter?'

The match burned my fingers, and I threw it away. 'When the hell did *you* start smoking?' I said.

She stared at me unperturbed. 'About the time you started swearing, I expect,' she said. 'When the war started.' Her face became a little sad. 'Or perhaps after that – when people began to get killed. Did you know Tommy Colney was dead?'

'When?'

'I don't know when. On the Somme. Arthur Stokes, too. And Henry Benson came home wounded.'

The good humour I'd begun to recover disappeared again. I didn't like the way people in England dwelt on this sort of thing. It made the war an ugly personal thing that involved me. It was much better to do what we did on a squadron and pretend it hadn't happened. Whenever there was an empty chair in the mess we always all politely ignored it as if it weren't there and the next night when it was filled by a replacement everything came all right again.

There was an enormous quality of sadness about her, however, that even I could feel, the everlasting female grieving over male stupidity. 'It's a horrid war,' she said. She took the matches from me and lit her cigarette with such aplomb and skill I felt a little boy in front of her.

As she blew out the smoke, she managed a big smile that seemed a little unreal. 'How about you?' she said. 'Got a girl yet?'

'Only you. Who else'd have me?'

'Plenty.'

'With a face like mine?'

'Nothing wrong with your face that I can see,' she said. 'It's a good face. An honest face.'

'Even if not too clever.'

'Sometimes it even looks clever.'

'Too many knobs and bumps on it to be good-looking, though,' I said, hoping she'd tell me it wasn't like that at all.

She didn't, though. She was far too honest to flatter. 'They give it character,' she said.

'But not beauty.'

She gave a little frown. 'Martin Falconer,' she said, and the way it came out made me feel about fifteen. 'You've got to stop running yourself down in this way. You make yourself out to be stupid, ugly and clumsy. You're nothing of the sort. You're quite a person. Or hadn't you noticed?'

She seemed ancient in her wisdom, though she was actually younger than I was and once more I felt that our relationship was suddenly all wrong. I'd always got on well with Jane. Once I'd been in love with her sister, with the soulful love of a little boy, and when she'd rejected me for my brother I'd suddenly noticed that Jane was growing up too. When I'd had my first leave from France I'd realized she was already a young woman. Now she seemed mature and confident, in a way that I still hadn't managed. While she at seventeen was already grown-up, at eighteen and a half I still felt just a child.

Only at home, though, I thought, seeking consolation. Only at home! On a squadron it didn't matter if you blushed when you made a *faux pas*

46

or said something stupid or almost choked over the whisky someone had shoved into your fist to steady you after some particularly nerve-racking experience. There, it only mattered that you could do what was expected of you with an aeroplane and that you had the courage to do it even when the sky was full of flying pieces of metal.

We were both very quiet as we finished the journey. It was almost as though Jane had sensed what was passing through my mind and was carefully avoiding bringing it into the open, because I suspected she'd also caught on to the difference between us. Because we'd held hands in the dark on my last leave and I'd fumbled a clumsy kiss as I'd gone back to France, she was being gentle with my emotions and letting them sort themselves out without help.

As we rolled up to the door of the farm, the gravel crunching under the wheels, she turned and smiled at me and suddenly I felt the situation was much easier. She'd made it much easier.

As we stopped she shivered and pulled her collar tighter. 'Come in and have a cup of tea,' she suggested. 'It's cold and I've got some tea-cakes and we can toast them in front of the fire.'

It dawned on me that the tea-cakes meant more to me than Jane and I felt better immediately.

'Done,' I said.

As I threw the bicycle against the browning winter forsythia that grew against the porch, I saw a horse tethered near the stackyard and the old stableman coming out with a bag of oats for it. I wondered whose it was because it was one of the handsomest beasts I'd seen for a long time. Jane had missed it in her haste to get out of the wind, and I followed her inside, hoping it wasn't anybody so important I'd shrivel up.

The winter afternoon was coming to an end and the hall was full of shadow. Jane's mother came out of the kitchen, carrying a tea pot.

'Martin!' she said. 'I didn't know you were home!' She paused long enough to beam at me, then led the way to the sitting-room. 'Come inside, Jane,' she went on. 'You've arrived just in time. There's someone to see you.'

I could have sworn Jane blushed but it was hard to tell in the shadow, and then she was standing in the doorway, the light from the lamp on her face, a slow smile of sheer delight spreading across her features.

I followed her into the sitting-room and stopped dead, staring at the man just rising from a chair by the fireplace. He was elegant and poised and made me feel lumpish, badly dressed and awkward. I seemed pushed out, gauche and far too young, and I was disgusted with him.

'What the hell are *you* doing here?' I blurted out indignantly.

Chapter 3

Sykes had obviously moved fast. Even with the advantage of a motor car he'd made good time to get from Hathersett by horse, especially looking as he did. He was wearing immaculate breeches and boots and a hacking jacket that seemed to have been built around him.

'Ludo,' Jane said, her eyes surprisingly bright. 'This is Martin. Martin Falconer.'

Sykes came forward, a faint smile in his eyes, and held out his hand gravely, as if he'd never seen me before. 'Delighted,' he said. 'How nice to meet you.'

Jane turned to me, blushing furiously. 'Martin, this is Ludo.'

The protest that was on the point of strangling me burst out at last. '*Ludo?*' I said indignantly. 'That's not Ludo! That's Bill Sykes!'

It was her turn to stare. 'You know each other?'

'He's been getting in my way for months,' I said. 'Two nights ago, in fact, I nearly ploughed him down.'

'But this is…' Jane was looking from one to the other of us now, bewildered, and Sykes' solemn face cracked.

'Tell you a secret, Brat,' he said to me. 'My name's not *really* Bill. It's Coe Ludovic Wilfred Bartelott-Dyveton-Sykes.'

'I don't believe it. Nobody could ever have a name like that.'

'No gettin' away from it. On my birth certifi-cate.'

'C. L. W. B. D. Sykes,' I said. 'I've seen it on your kit. I thought at first it was a chemical formula.'

Sykes was smiling broadly now. 'Protested as soon as I was old enough,' he said. 'Too late by then, though. What are *you* doing here?'

'I live here.' I gestured. 'Over there. A couple of miles away.'

'At Fynling! Of course!'

'And you at Hathersett.' I stared at him, light suddenly dawning. 'Gosh,' I said. 'You're not one of the Bartelott-Dyveton-Sykes from that great palace of a place there, are you?'

''Fraid I am. Son and heir actually.'

'Good Lord!' I felt like a poor relation.

'Doesn't matter,' Sykes said cheerfully. 'We get on quite well with the proletariat.'

Suddenly things began to click into place. The horse outside. Things he'd mentioned. Jane's evasiveness and her father's uncertainty. He'd obviously been coming over to Fynling often.

'Met a cracking girl down that way,' he'd said on the train, and as I looked quickly at Jane I saw she hadn't taken her eyes off him since she'd entered the room. I looked back at Sykes again and for the first time since I'd met him in France I realized that he wasn't the mature man I'd always imagined but someone who wasn't really very much older than I was – perhaps twenty-two or twenty-three – but who was so much more adult because he was poised and worldly. I couldn't imagine Sykes ever falling over the carpet – as I did regularly – when he was trying to make a grand entrance into a room full of girls.

'That your horse outside?' I said.

'Yes. Rode over. Thought I might as well.' He looked at Jane. 'Didn't expect *him* to be here, of course,' he said to her. 'Badly brought up, shouldn't wonder. Gets in the way a lot. Specially in the air.'

He glanced at Jane's mother and his smile died. 'Came over with some bad news, actually.'

I knew what it was without asking. 'You're going back to France?'

Sykes nodded and I saw Jane's face fall. 'Given me a squadron,' he went on. 'Rather a good show, really. Didn't expect one.'

I felt the bottom fall out of my world. Sykes had become everything to me. Father-confessor, co-conspirator in the forming of plans for aerial combat against the edicts of the authorities at head-quarters, the superior officer who was always ready to try out the half-baked new ideas I thought of, the one man who'd never treated me – as some of the older men were in the habit of doing – as a schoolboy who had to be favoured. I couldn't imagine the squadron without him.

'When?' I asked.

'Immediately. Telegram came.'

'Ask for me,' I said impulsively, almost begging. 'I'd like to be in the same mob.'

Sykes gave me that brilliant smile of his, that smile that was always sufficient reward for the effort to the man who picked up his coat when he dropped it, the mechanic who laboured all night over his engine so he could be in the air at first light, the tender driver who conveyed him to the station. It was a gift of charming people such as I'd never have if I lived a million years because it came from generations of Sykes males getting people to do things for them. There had probably been Sykeses and Bartelotts smiling at serfs at the courts of King Harold before William of Normandy even began to cast covetous eyes across the Channel.

'Don't forget,' I went on. 'Ask for me.'

'Thought of it already,' Sykes said.

I was so overwhelmed that he wanted me in his squadron I had quite failed to notice that Jane's eyes were big and moist. They were suddenly so full of sadness I became aware at once that I'd stayed too long.

'Thanks,' I said. 'Thanks, Bill.' For a moment I wondered if I ought to call him 'Sir Bill' or 'Lord Bill' because I knew there was a title around some-where at Hathersett, but it didn't seem to fit him and I settled for the normal.

'I'll be getting home,' I said.

'Aren't you staying for tea?' I noticed it wasn't Jane who asked but her mother.

'No,' I said. 'I'll be off. I haven't seen my parents yet.'

Somehow I got out of the door without falling over the step, and as I mounted the bicycle and pedalled home through the dusk I felt myself surrounded by black treachery. Somehow, I felt, Jane should have told me, her parents should have told me, my parents should have written. Then gradually commonsense took over and I realized that a gauche boy not nineteen and never noted for saying the right thing at the right time was no match for a wealthy young man of the world like Sykes, and I felt better enough even to marvel that it had been Jane – Jane whom I'd thought I was in love with myself – who'd captured his affection. It made me feel almost related to him and I was delighted, and my resentment vanished because it was clear Jane had forgotten me in the first moment she'd seen Sykes.

Because I, too, thought there was no one in the world like him, I could hardly blame her for thinking the same.

–

When I got back on the Sunday night, Sykes was with the Major, organizing his departure. The klaxon that sounded the Zeppelin alarm had gone so that there were machines in the air. It was too late for me to join them so I wandered down to the field to see what was happening. It was cold so I'd slipped on a jersey and I stood by the flarepath staring at the sky and catching the acrid smell of burning paraffin in my nostrils as the smoke wafted down the line of lights.

'Anything been seen?' I asked the flight-sergeant in charge.

'Not a thing, sir. The Hun's probably doing a practice trip over Cuxhaven and someone tipped the wink to London. You know what they're like there.'

I knew.

'There's a bunch of new chaps arrived, sir,' the flight-sergeant went on. 'Just came in. To take the place of Mr McSpadden, Mr Graves and Mr Williamson.'

I nodded, not really listening. Even now, even back on the field, I was still a little bewildered that Jane could have changed her mind so fast. I couldn't find it in me to blame her, however, and I decided

I was more mature than I'd realized. I'd been able to face the fact that she thought more of someone else than she did of me – without missing a meal, I'd noticed – and I decided it was simply old age and cynicism catching up.

While I was staring down the line of flares, I heard voices behind me and one of them sounded vaguely familiar. I'd heard hundreds, thousands, of voices in the last eighteen months but this one seemed to dig back into the past, and as I turned round I knew why. A burly second-lieutenant was staring at me, grinning.

'Well, if it isn't young Falconer,' he said. 'Thought I recognized you. You look a bit different now from when I first met you at school.' He turned to the other young men with him, also second-lieutenants with brand new overcoats and pips.

· 'At school with this chap,' he said, indicating me arrogantly with a cock of his thumb. 'He was one of the little toads in the second form when I left. Used to object when I knocked him about a bit.' He grinned at me. 'I bet you don't remember me, do you, young Falconer?'

Not half I don't, I thought. A lot of other things hung together suddenly, too – a familiar face and a bullying manner in Fynling and the memory of misery at school. His name was Catlow and, with his fashionable toothbrush moustache and the cap with the wire removed to give him a dashing 'Gorblimey' air, he looked as slimy now as he did then. He had often made my life miserable with his overbearing bumptiousness and big fists.

'Had to give you a thick ear more than once, didn't I?' he said. 'What are you doing here? Just arrived?'

I looked up at him and said nothing and he went on loudly.

'Have to be a bit more careful here, y'know. This isn't school and we're not playing cricket.'

'No,' I said gravely, trying to look like Sykes did when someone irritated him. 'So they tell me. How about you?'

'Pilot,' he said with heavy self-importance. 'This is Peckett and this is Bull. Off the same course.'

I nodded at the other two and he went on cheerfully. 'How about you? Airfield security?'

I don't know what he thought I was because I was without a cap and wore slacks instead of breeches and, wearing the jersey instead of a tunic, there was no insignia of rank showing.

'I suppose you'd call it that,' I said. 'Been flying long?'

'Yes. Gave up a good job in the city to do my bit.'

'And now you've come to show the Germans a thing or two?'

'Not half. Those old Huns'll have to watch their step now, eh, Peckett?'

Peckett, who was a tall pale-eyed young man, didn't seem half so confident as Catlow and only managed a wan smile in the glow of the flares. But Catlow was never lacking in confidence or bounce. At school, he had always been in the habit of announcing his successes before they'd arrived, and despite previous failures, had always seemed surprised when they failed to materialize. How he'd become a pilot I had no idea but I suspected he was a rotten one.

While he was telling the uninterested Peckett just how he proposed to win the war, I learned from Bull, a thick-shouldered man who seemed quite unimpressed by him, that they had joined up six months before and had about six and a half hours' flying to their credit. I felt I was going to enjoy meeting Catlow officially when the time came.

Nothing was seen of the Zeppelins, of course, and when I returned to the mess, Sykes was there making his farewells. As I entered, Catlow, Peckett and Bull were standing alongside him, stiff and ill-at-ease as became newcomers in front of a man with two medal ribbons, a wound stripe and three pips on his shoulders. Sykes called me across.

'Hello, Ludo,' I said with great deliberation.

He gave me a funny look at the name but, to my delight, he put his arm round my shoulder. I could see Catlow's eyes almost popping out of his head at the inch of ribbon under my wings.

'This is the chap who'll be taking over the flight,' Sykes said, and it was news to me because it was the first I'd heard of it. But I was pleased all the same, if only for the look on Catlow's face.

Sykes went on briskly. 'Take no notice of the youthful innocence,' he said. 'You'll learn a lot from him. There's nothing he doesn't know about flying. He's been in it from the very beginning and he's full of ideas.' He turned to me. 'I'm off tomorrow, Brat,' he went on. 'Things are waking up a bit in France. I'll ask for you as soon as I get there. For the moment though, you'd better take these chaps up in the morning and see what they can do.'

He left early the next day and I got up at dawn especially to see him off. Despite the hour, he looked as though he'd stepped out of a fashion magazine or one of those advertisements tailors were always putting in the newspapers with tailor's-dummy officers waving a swagger stick and wearing puttees that never managed to look like the ones I wore. The mess waiters were hovering near, looking as though they'd been orphaned or something, because they all thought the world of Sykes.

He was just shaking hands all round as I arrived and he beamed as he saw me. 'Nice of you to get up,' he said.

'No trouble. Couldn't sleep.'

He seemed a little thoughtful. 'Think I owe you a sort of apology,' he went on.

'Me? Why?'

'Jane.'

'Oh! That!'

'Well' – he shrugged – 'from what she tells me now, it seems you'd always imagined she was *your* girl.'

'Yes, I did, I suppose.' There was no point in not being honest.

'No hard feelings, I hope?'

It wouldn't have made much difference what I thought. There was nothing about me that could compare with Sykes' attributes.

''Course not.'

'Cracking girl,' he said. He shook hands. 'Must be off. Take care of yourself, Brat.'

'Yes, Mummy! I'll be careful.'

I watched the tender take him off to the station. I'd not really got to know him properly in France, but in England we'd become surprisingly close friends, considering the difference in background and age. I felt bereft and decided that while I was feeling so down in the dumps I'd make a meal of it and take Catlow up and find out how bad he was.

He was awful.

'How many hours' flying have you had?' I asked him.

'Thirty-odd,' he said.

I didn't believe him for a minute.

'Let's have a look at your log book.'

He changed his tune sharply. 'Sorry,' he said. 'Bit mixed up. Thought you said – er – it's seven.'

'The way *you* fly it could well be seven minutes.' I was unnecessarily cruel with him but he'd never hesitated to be cruel to me at school and I was still low in spirits. 'You need practice. You'll have to get more hours in.'

He obviously hated me telling him what to do. 'It'll be enough,' he said.

'Why? Expecting to get on the staff?'

I could tell from the look on his face that I was right.

'Suppose you don't,' I said. 'Suppose something goes wrong. It'll do no harm to know what to do, will it?'

–

Inevitably, because I wanted to be with Sykes and because Sykes wanted it, too, the powers that existed at the War Office decided otherwise. He was taking over the squadron of a man who'd been killed and he had to take it over just as it was. And because I'd been in England the appropriate length of time after a tour of duty in France they deemed it wiser to keep me there. You can ask for him, they told Sykes, when you need a replacement; but at the same time they told me, you can join him when you've done your tour of duty as an instructor and not before. The chances of the two coinciding seemed pretty slender.

But the war in the air in France was changing subtly. The superiority that the British held at the beginning of the Somme had been lost again as the Germans had produced their first Albatros, a shark-like machine with blunt square wings which was said to be faster than and could outclimb anything we possessed. It was strong and sturdy, they said, and could dive like a bomb, and in the hands of a good pilot could be incredibly dangerous.

And they had some good men, too.

Immelman, who'd more than once put the fear of God into me over Douai on my first tour, was dead, killed in the early days of the Somme in a fight with a lumbering FE2b. The Fee crew had claimed to have shot him down but the story had got round that the interrupter gear which enabled him to fire his gun forward had run away and he had shot off his propeller and the machine had fallen to pieces with the vibration. Boelcke, who had wrought so much damage with him among British planes, was dead, too, killed in a mid-air collision, but no one had any doubts that there would be someone new along soon to take their places, and already it was being said that the Germans were organizing their best pilots into one or two elite squadrons which could do untold damage working together, instead of spreading them in penny numbers along the whole front. It seemed a good idea to me.

Not that it had *all* gone the way of the Germans, though. There was a Nottingham man called Albert Ball who was not much older than I was but seemed to be getting himself talked about a lot in the messes, and a few others I'd heard of and envied, and there were said to be new machines on the way that would make the Germans sit up and watch what they were doing. I only hoped I'd be in France when they arrived.

Christmas came round again, the third Christmas of the war, when in August 1914 they'd been saying it would be all over by the first, and I grew bored to tears flying round the countryside with advanced pupils. Catlow was still with us and we all felt sure he was just waiting a posting to some prearranged staff job. He was no better than when he'd first arrived. He was ham-fisted and clearly hadn't that fine instinctive sense that made a good pilot. Peckett and Bull were better but they'd all been poorly trained. Perhaps it wasn't their fault because training methods and conditions were chaotic and every instructor had different methods, and every pupil learned to fly a different way so that it was almost impossible for one man to take over another's pupils. The need for setting up some standards seemed so great, in fact, I submitted a report on the subject which seemed to impress the Major.

'You know what you've probably done?' he said gaily. 'You've probably worked youself a senior instructor's job for the rest of the war.'

I was horrified. I still only wanted to join Sykes.

'A man who can write a report like that isn't likely to pass unnoticed,' the Major went on. 'They'll probably ask you to set up a new system here.'

I gulped. 'Then I'd like to withdraw the paper, sir,' I said. 'I want to go back to France.'

He grinned. 'Don't worry,' he said. 'I'll try to keep the identity of the writer dark.'

I was growing very frustrated by now with instructing and slipped home whenever I could. But it was no longer quite the same. Jane was as friendly as ever but she'd changed inevitably.

We'd been good friends long before I'd imagined I'd fallen in love with her, however, and we still managed to take long walks along the wide Norfolk beaches, sometimes when the North Sea mists came rolling in and you had to know the place well to prevent yourself getting lost. There was rime on the grass in the fields behind and it was so cold we had to walk fast, talking invariably about Sykes. I'd had a few letters from him hastily scrawled on the backs of message sheets and a few from Jane who was clearly in much closer touch with him than I was, and it appeared he'd got himself another medal – from the Belgians this time. It wasn't hard to talk, because we were both fond of Sykes for entirely different reasons.

The winter dragged on, endless grey skies and rain that reduced flying to nothing. It was a drab period, sad and full of gloom. The offensive on the Somme had failed to break the German line and the disappointment had spread to every corner of the country and everyone seemed to be waking up to the fact that the war was different from what they'd ever expected. The bands that had still been playing in the streets the previous year had disappeared, broken up for the most part so that their members could fill the appalling gaps caused by the casualties, and there was a sort of sullen obstinacy about that early spring of 1917 because suddenly no one could see the end of the war, and disillusionment had set in.

Once I went over to Hathersett Hall with Jane. It was an imposing Georgian mansion situated in a park of several hundred acres, its architectural style a little frigid for my taste but impressive by any standard. The interior contained portraits by Gainsborough and Reynolds, and landscapes by Hobbema and the Dutch masters and, though I knew nothing about them, they were good enough to take my breath away.

Sykes' people were just like Sykes himself. His father was a retired cavalry colonel recalled to service and running a training camp in the north of England, and his mother was a vague regal kindly woman who made me feel completely at home. They shortened Sykes' name, Ludovic, to 'Lulu' among the family and they obviously adored Jane and clearly approved of her. To my surprise, I found Sykes had talked to them about me, and I was strangely flattered that he should, and felt that I was moving among the mighty. There was a young cousin there about Jane's age I fell heavily for. Her name was Charlotte but everyone called her Charley and she completely charmed me, as in a strange sort of way, they all did – as though they were acting the role of French aristocrats on the way to the guillotine, brave and full of dignity and humour in the face of danger. The family had already been decimated by the war because so many of them were in the services, and in the little room where Sykes' mother did her sewing, the mantelpiece was covered with photographs of men in uniform whom I learned were all cousins and nephews and uncles who had given their lives. Then I realized that they weren't acting a role at all but had behaved throughout their history as they were behaving now. They were a privileged group, and they paid for their privilege by offering their lives when their country was in danger.

Once I met Charley in London and we had a lively week-end of shows and tea-dances. She was gay and brittle and full of all the up-to-date things to say and do, and we thoroughly enjoyed ourselves.

'I'm a rotten dancer,' I pointed out as we struggled through a two-step.

'I've noticed,' she said cheerfully, 'Lulu's terrific.'

I knew he would be, of course.

'I'm not too bad on waltzes,' I said.

'Same here. With knobs on. Old-fashioned, but it doesn't matter. You get used to them in the end – like wooden legs.'

We even got romantic, holding hands on the Embankment, but it was freezing cold and a bit discouraging.

'Do you like girls?' Charley asked me in her clear high Roedean voice.

'On the whole,' I said, 'they frighten me to death.'

She giggled. 'I've never been kissed by a pilot,' she observed helpfully, and when we went to see 'The Maid of the Mountains', which was all the rage just then, and the hero sang his song about 'At seventeen he falls in love quite madly with eyes of tender blue, at twenty-one he's got it rather badly with eyes of a different hue', I realized it applied to me. Whoever had written those lines was quite a shrewd judge of adolescence.

While we were in London, someone introduced me to Albert Ball. He was a reserved young man, short and unprepossessing but with bright dark eyes and a keen jaw. He seemed uncomplicated and by no means intellectual and he said if I wished he'd try to pull a few strings and get me posted to 56 Squadron where he was going and which was coming to be considered rather special because it had a whole bunch of experienced pilots. I thanked him but said I was still hoping to join Sykes.

From time to time I got an opportunity to fly different machines, some of them awful, one or two of them good like the Bristol Scout, which was not only a sweet little machine to handle but a beautiful machine to look at.

One day I flew over to Joyce Green to pick up a new one. The Wing Fighting Instructor there was a man called McCudden who had gone to France in 1914 as an air mechanic and was now an officer with three medals. I watched him take up a Bristol Scout and do six loops in a row with it. He had a lot to say about fighting in France and I was able to pick up a few tips. He had some good ideas about instructing, too, and some good pupils, one of them, an Irishman called Mannock, being particularly impressive, though someone told me he was far too old to be a pilot and could only see out of one eye.

I was almost frantic to get back to France by this time and only the occasional alarms when the Germans were supposed to be approaching London brought any excitement. They all fizzled out as false, though, and the story went around that the Germans had called off the Zeppelins. Too many had been lost because of bad weather and they were now said to be developing a giant new bomber to do the job instead and were merely doing reconnaissance for when they were ready.

At the beginning of March, we were given a few Sopwith Pups for training and we all got a chance of trying our hands out on them, a few of the older hands even doing patrols, and I saw Bull watching me with dour envy as the Major sent me up to look out for the Germans. Peckett seemed unenthusiastic, a curious pale character of a man who seemed to leave no impression on anyone, while Catlow was frankly indifferent. It was clear now that he had no wish to do any more than he was doing at that moment, and Jane had heard stories in Fynling which confirmed the rumours that strings were being pulled to get him posted to the staff or as a permanent instructor and I guessed that was the reason for his comfortable self-satisfaction.

Nothing ever happened on the patrols, of course, except that one day I saw an aeroplane way below me and stalked it for what seemed hours. Whatever it was, it was faster than a Pup and I never caught it, but I saw it several times after that and became convinced that it was one of the high-flying German reconnaissance planes we'd heard of, sneaking across the Channel to take photographs of London Docks with those wonderful cameras they had. I began to wait for him and in the end he became an obsession.

I began to ask the other pilots about him and even began to visit other squadrons in search of information. But I seemed to be the only one who'd ever spotted him, and people began to laugh and ask if I'd seen Old Faithful lately. Finally it became a matter of pride to find out just who the intruder was, so that I began to fly higher and higher in the hope of catching him unawares.

One day I actually got the Pup up to 18,500 feet which was about as high as anyone ever got one and I began to think I was pretty good. I was just basking in self-satisfaction when I saw Old Faithful below me on my left and I banked round at once after him. The Pup had reached its limit, though, and as I turned on to a new course I lost 500 feet at once in the thin air and had to start the slow deliberate climb upwards again. But I had my eye on the other machine now and I had learned long since in France that height put the odds in your favour every time.

There was a lot of cirrocumulus about and the other aeroplane started to dodge in and out among it, which made me more certain than ever that he was a German. I decided to take no chance and fired the gun to warm it up.

Old Faithful turned again, and again I lost height as I turned with him. But I had manoeuvred behind him and above his tail now and I was right in the eye of the sun as I began a long steep glide towards him. I still couldn't make out what the other machine was but I had long since made out the black crosses on his wings and decided he was in for a nasty surprise. He turned slightly and I turned with him. I was drawing nicely close to him now, only 500 yards away and approaching fast, and I'd still not been seen. The observer was hanging over the side, probably using a camera, and had never looked up.

Four hundred yards, three, two, one, seventy-five, fifty. Now! I pressed the trigger. The gun barked once then stopped and I shot helplessly past within a matter of yards of the German. I was livid with rage as I saw the observer look up, startled, then bang the pilot on the shoulder and grab for his gun. The pilot, who must have been enjoying the view, swung the machine over in a bank and fell out of the sky in a steep dive, while I tried to follow him, banging on the cocking handle of the gun to drive the cartridge home, cursing and furious, but unable to do a thing about it. All I could do was follow him down in the hope of frightening him into crashing into the sea, but he was far too old a hand for that and he levelled out not far above the waves and fled across the Channel, while I could only weave about above him, keeping out of the way of the streams of bullets that were snapped off in my direction by the observer every time I came within range.

I landed with a splitting headache from the altitude and was in a foul temper with myself and with the armourer who'd serviced the gun. The jam was caused by a *faulty* round and I was furious that he hadn't noticed it because that sort of thing could get you killed if it happened at the wrong time. The armourer was cheerful about it. He was a little mad,

I think. He was called Gumbell – Gum Boil to his friends inevitably – and he had a habit of playing a fiddle outside his hut at night, because he played it so badly his hut-mates refused to allow him to play it inside.

'It wasn't my fault, sir,' he insisted.

'Whose was it then?' I demanded.

'Well, I didn't make that there bullet.'

'No.' I had to agree. 'But you made up the belt. From now on I'll make 'em up myself and I'll check every cartridge.'

I went to the office to make my report. Catlow was inside with Peckett and Bull and he was looking a little green about the gills. The Major looked up as I arrived.

'See anything?' he asked.

'One aeroplane, sir. The chap I've been chasing. I'll be up there tomorrow again in case he comes back.'

He grinned. 'Oh, no, you won't,' he said. 'I've got a job for you with these chaps here.'

I looked at the other three. I still didn't hit it off with Catlow and I couldn't imagine enjoying anything he was involved in.

'What is it?' I asked.

'France,' the Major said.

'What!' I suddenly understood the look on Catlow's face. '*France!*'

The Major laughed. 'They've suddenly noticed all those applications you've been putting in,' he said. 'You've been posted. You're to pick up new Pups and cross the Channel to Rochy-le-Moutrou.'

'What's the squadron?' I said.

He told me and my heart fell to my boots. 'That's not Sykes'.'

'What did you expect?' the Major said with a smile. 'You made too much of a fuss about joining him. You ought to know that the powers that be only exist to thwart people like you and me. What you should have done was apply to go to any squadron *but* Sykes'.'

I went off in a fury and wrote another application. It was properly in triplicate and in good Service language but it was also full of rage and sarcasm. The Major glanced at it then he grinned and handed it back to me. 'Sorry,' he said. 'I'm not going to put it through. If I did they'd court martial me and probably shoot you. There's nothing for it, Falconer. You're going where they've told you to go. You can do what you like about transferring when you get there. But there's nothing I can do here.'

Chapter 4

We flew to France via Dover, halting to refuel and have lunch at Lympne before setting our course from Dover Castle. We landed at Marquis, near Boulogne, in time for tea. I'd had to watch Catlow carefully because he was constantly straggling. He'd spent a solid three hours on the telephone from the village pub the evening before we'd left, and Bull, who'd been there with Peckett, said his indignant bleating had been heard by everyone in the place. Clearly his plans had gone awry and he was making hurried shifts to get some help.

When we landed he said he'd been having trouble with his machine but I caught the flight-sergeant's glance and suspected it was just an excuse and that he wasn't looking forward to France. Shortly afterwards we flew on to a place called Petit Snythe, and stayed the night there and went on the following morning to Rochy-le-Moutrou. It was the ominous date of 1 April 1917 – April Fool's Day.

Rochy was a triangular-shaped field and as I approached I could see some FE2bs on the ground that indicated we were sharing it with another squadron. There was an awkward line of trees at one end, but I dropped over them without trouble. Catlow, who was straggling again, only just missed them, however, got into a wobble and made a bad landing that stood his machine on its nose. Almost immediately a Crossley tender came hurtling out from among the huts, bouncing over the grass, and stopped alongside him. I saw a tall man get out and Catlow standing very straight and stiff while he got what was clearly a wigging.

Then the Crossley went across to Peckett and Bull and I saw them also standing stiff and silent. When I saw it coming across to me, I decided *I* wasn't going to do any standing stiff and silent and deliberately turned my back to take my coat off.

As the Crossley screeched to a halt behind me, I heard a loud voice as the door slammed. 'When are you new pilots going to get some training?' it said. 'I'm damned if I...'

As I turned, the voice faded at once and I saw a big red-faced man staring at the ribbon under my wings.

'What did you get that for?' he demanded.

'Flying, sir,' I said. I was always much better at standing up to angry officers than I was to girls.

'Oh!' He began to calm down considerably. 'This your second tour of duty?'

The anger died out of his face immediately and he turned back to the Crossley. 'Better let me have your papers and all the rest of the nonsense,' he growled. 'I'm the C.O. My name's Latta.'

He climbed back into the tender and disappeared. He hadn't impressed me very much.

I walked across to Catlow who'd now been joined by Peckett and Bull. His bad landing wasn't anything unusual – some of the most successful fliers wrecked as many British machines as German – but he was still red in the face from what had been said to him.

'My God,' he said, when he saw me. 'That was a bit rich!'

'I shouldn't worry too much,' I said. 'He's probably in need of a bit of leave.'

My guess was a good one. Latta had been out far too long and was tired and suddenly overworked as the front woke up with the better weather of spring. He was in control of himself when we arrived.

'We've had rather a knock,' he said as I handed over the papers. 'We're under strength and now we've lost three men in one week. That's a lot. The

Germans opposite are too damned good for us with these new Albatroses.'

'Which new Albatroses?' I asked.

'DIIIs. They're hot stuff – much faster than the DIs. Pups can barely stand up to them and hitting 'em for six gets harder all the time.'

It was news to me and a bit of a blow because we'd thought the Pups were first-rate machines which had been brought out as the answer to DIs.

Latta was pawing through the scattered papers on his desk now, his whole manner harassed and short-tempered. 'You'll be in A flight, with Catlow,' he said. 'The others'll be in B. You'll be deputy leader. Do you know this part of the line?'

I said I did and he nodded. 'You'd better take them all over straight away then. Let 'em have a look at it. But don't take any chances. We've stopped solitary patrols. No one goes over alone these days. We go in twos and threes.'

As we turned away, he called us back. 'Oh, and keep a watch towards Douai. That's where trouble comes from.'

I remembered the Fokkers that had bothered me the previous year. 'It always did,' I said.

He seemed anxious to appear keen and interested. 'They're a painted lot,' he said. 'They daub their machines all colours. I'm told it's so they can distinguish each other in the air. Leader's a chap called Richthofen.'

Catlow's machine hadn't been much damaged and, after lunch, with a new propeller it was fit to fly. Catlow looked nervous, though, and I told him to keep close to me and do what I did.

'Always keep a look-out up there.' I jerked a hand at the watery sun. 'Watch it all the time. Not just when you're bored but always. Shove a thumb in front of your eye when you look up. It kills the glare and allows you to see. It might be a black spot. It might be a pale white cross, it might be a flash as the sun catches a pair of wings. But if you see anything, look again and, if you're sure, let me know.'

Catlow looked sullen. He'd never enjoyed having someone as young as I was tell him what to do and he still hadn't got over the fact that he'd been swept into the net of the war while his relatives were fighting tooth and nail to save him. I didn't intend being merciful with him, however, and jabbed a hand at the tails of their machines. 'And keep one eye on those,' I went on. 'Keep looking until your neck aches, because if anybody comes at you, that's where he'll come from.'

Catlow seemed to think what I was telling them was a lot of nonsense but I hoped for his sake that he was taking notice, because I was taking no chances myself. I'd long since taken the opportunity of making a few additions to my machine. I didn't like the windscreen with its padded edge because it spoiled my vision, and I'd had it taken off and replaced with another that was curved and gave me a better view. In addition, I'd also spent the lunch hour pasting maps of the region for thirty miles either side of the line on to thick squares of cardboard and slotting them into a holder alongside my seat. I'd learned that survival depended on care and preparation and, in view of the reputation of the new German Albatroses, it seemed a good idea to do what I could to narrow the gap between us with a little forethought.

The Le Rhône was still warm and it sounded good as it roared into life, the Pup quivering under the stress of its power. I'd learned in England that trying to handle the Pup in thick leather regulation gloves was like trying to play cricket with a feather, and I'd searched London for a pair of finer ones that allowed a more sensitive touch.

As the rumble of wheels stopped and we became airborne, I glanced back. Bull was close up on me, grimly holding his position. Peckett was just behind, but Catlow was wandering away already. He seemed congenitally incapable of flying in formation. I waved him fiercely into position but I had to throttle back to allow him to catch up before we headed for the line. The brown stain of the trenches had not changed much since the last time I'd seen it but, as always, I was not emotionally moved by the sight of it. It had been there a long time now, a great scar on the earth running all the way from Switzerland to the sea, and it didn't concern me. My base was in green meadows and my battlefield was up here in a clear sky where it was swept clean by the wind after every struggle.

There had been a lot of fighting in the last year and the ground below seemed to be honeycombed with shell-holes, all filled with water. The artillery fire had shattered dykes and streams and turned it into a desolation of mud so that I wondered how men lived in it. As I stared down at it I heard a different sound from the monotonous roar of the engine and glanced quickly round, knowing at once what it was. Three hundred yards away on the same level several puff balls of black smoke hung in the sky. Anti-aircraft fire was always a little unnerving. On the ground, shells never seemed to have the same importance because you always knew they were fired at random into the blue at anyone who happened to be in the target area.

In the air, it was different because it was very clear they were aimed directly at you, and it gave them a personal spiteful effect.

Even as I stared at them, the next shell burst with an almighty crack just ahead of us and almost immediately I saw Catlow swing nervously away. He was several hundred yards off to the right as I waved him back again, furious with him, and I changed course towards him, partly to put the anti-aircraft gunners off their target and partly to let him catch up. The proportion of casualties from anti-aircraft fire was always small but I'd once seen a direct hit on an old slow-flying BE – just a flash and a puff of smoke, then fragments of wood and fluttering fabric and two dark shapes twisting and turning as they fell. It *could* happen and I never treated anti-aircraft fire with contempt, but the best thing was not to change direction so much as to change height, a thing that wasn't so noticeable from below.

The puff balls fell behind and I flew north towards Lens then turned south without crossing the line and headed over the misty ponds of the River Scarpe, constantly watching Catlow and changing course and height from time to time to put the gunners off. Finally I turned west into the wind towards Rochy-le-Moutrou. I'd seen a few aeroplanes about – a small group up near the sun and one or two small sliding spots low over the clouds, and the flash of wings in the east as the sun caught the varnished surface of a banking aeroplane – but none of them had approached us, and I'd kept well clear of them. Catlow, Peckett and Bull needed time to get acclimatized.

Back on the ground, already feeling the burning sensation of frostbite on my cheeks, I told Catlow what I thought of him. As usual, he was surly and rude. 'There were no Huns about,' he muttered. 'The sky was empty.'

'If that's what you think,' I pointed out, 'then you're dafter than I thought. I saw plenty.'

He shrugged. 'Not that it matters. I don't expect to be here long. I'll be away before the month's out.'

So that was it. His panic call for help had clearly brought results and his plans were made and he felt he could afford to be casual. I hoped he was right. As I turned away I heard him muttering to Peckett. 'Blasted ribbon-hunters,' he was saying contemptuously. 'I think he was drawing it out a bit, personally.'

The mess was in a farmhouse and was comfortable enough, but it was in a gloomy mood that evening and it seemed to me that they'd got the wind-up. They'd lost a few men in the past few weeks and nobody had done much to snap them out of their mood. Latta was obviously past his best, and the flight commanders, Orgill, Porteous and Le Petit, were no better. They were all in need of a rest, all of them pale-faced and wearing a stricken look that was a mixture of strain and outrage, which I guessed had come from seeing too many of their men disappear and having too little encouragement from Latta. The whole atmosphere of the mess was heavy, and the only member who seemed to have any life left in him was a little Scot called Munro with an accent you could cut with a knife. He was only about five feet two with a great bony beak of a nose, but he seemed to have the guts of a lion. He'd been in France since 1914 and had to walk with two sticks because of wounds suffered as an infantryman, but his spirit was by no means impaired, and he was contemptuous of the others.

'Yon lot hae got the willies, laddie,' he told me. 'They see bogeys everywhere.'

'*Are* there bogeys everywhere?' I asked.

He grinned. 'Och, aye,' he said. 'Sure there are! The Circus, we call 'em. Painted like a lot o' harlots and led by a laddie in a red machine. The Bloody Red Baron we call him.'

'Are they good?'

He grinned again, clearly undisturbed. 'Hae they no' got the new Albatros?' he said. 'If ye see a machine wi' a V-shaped strut, laddie, watch out. It's yon new DIII. They've got two guns firing through the propeller against our one, so ye'll need to be gey careful wi' 'em.'

'Like you?'

He gave me a wan smile that suddenly betrayed a host of unspoken, fought-down fears. 'Aye, like me,' he said. 'Ah'm that careful these days, laddie, it hurts. Ah've been oot a long time, ye see, and Ah want tae gae hame tae Aberdeen eventually.'

The meal was eaten almost in silence. Munro made a few attempts at conversation but he got nowhere and almost everyone at the table seemed afflicted by deafness.

'It's no' just the Navy that's called the Silent Service,' he whispered.

It was a dreary meal, and the mess eventually lapsed into complete silence. Bull was eating dourly with his head down, while Catlow picked at his vegetables as though he'd found a worm in them.

'Pass the sauce, please,' Munro said suddenly in a loud voice and I swore I saw Le Petit jump.

'Ye've got tae mak' yersel' haird,' Munro said cheerfully to me, with a wink. 'Otherwise ye dinnae get noticed in the chatter.'

Le Petit, a gloomy-looking Guernseyman, glowered at him but Munro was unmoved.

While we were eating, Latta appeared to give out the orders for the next day. A and B flights were to furnish the duty patrols, with A doing the first and last and B the afternoon flight. I was to fly with Porteous and another man called Howarth while Bull, Peckett and Catlow were to spend their time improving their landings and in shooting at a target in the next field.

Munro was orderly officer the next morning and he was at breakfast in the ghostly half-lit mess when we appeared. 'Hard-boiled eggs again,' he snorted. 'They always gi'e me indigestion. They're an awfu' thing tae gae tae war on, mon.'

Snowflakes were whirling round us as we trudged to the hangars, wrapping scarves round our necks and fastening buckles and buttons in a faint morning light that was beginning to outline trees and farm buildings. The ground crew, swaddled and padded in balaclavas, mufflers, dungarees and mittens, broke into a shuffling run over the frozen turf to heave at wings and tail units with blue hands and split fingertips. They'd been up ages heating the oil in drums over stoves to pour into the engines so they'd start up when they were wanted.

'Watch yon Porteous, laddie,' Munro had whispered as I'd left the mess. 'He's so scared, he thinks he's got to show he's not. It makes things a wee bitty dangerous.'

I wasn't sure what he meant but as the engines started with bursts of blue smoke and we climbed into the sun that laid a brilliant orange stain over the Scarpe, I decided I'd be twice as alert. I wasn't nervous, only frozen. I'd done it all before and I knew I was no mug as a pilot by this time.

Bullecourt and Feuchy came up beneath us, shabby-looking and frosted in the early-morning sunshine. It was shining directly into our eyes now and picked up two FEs so that they looked like tinselled birdcages as they drifted over the lines. Just to the south I could see a BE2C doing an artillery shoot and I was thankful that I wasn't in it.

The inevitable snarl of anti-aircraft shells made me jump as it always did, but it made me sit up, too, more alert than before, with my eyes all round the sky, because the German gunners sometimes fired to indicate our position to their friends higher up or in the eye of the sun.

Porteous didn't seem to show any interest and it only served to make me more concerned. Whatever Porteous might or might not see, I was determined *I* wasn't going to miss anything, and I watched the rising sun keenly for any early-flying German who might be hiding down there.

Groups of clouds like cotton wool edged with gold lay in the distance, with brighter banks of cumulus behind them slab-sided and solid-looking. Porteous changed course and another BE drifted past below us, moving sideways in that crablike manner of all aeroplanes on a different course. We were at 15,000 feet now and I was petrified and wretched with the cold but I was still wishing that Porteous would try to get a little higher.

Near La Bassee, as another slow-flying BE drifted past, I saw the sun flash on a varnished wing to the east and knew there were aeroplanes there. Then I saw them heading for the BE below – just as Porteous began to rock his wings and point to them. Somehow it seemed too easy and I glanced upwards again. Sure enough there were four small dots above us, silver-grey and almost invisible against the upper sky.

But Porteous had already started down, firing far too soon so that the Germans below broke away in plenty of time. They were the new Albatroses, and the V-strut, spade tail and swept-back wings were clearly visible as they swung outwards. Instead of sticking together, both Porteous and Howarth swung out after them, and with the lighter wing-loading of the Pups which made them better than the Albatroses only at height, it seemed to me a stupid thing to do. But we were committed now, and a moment later we were really committed because I saw an all-red machine flash past me and caught the acrid smell of tracer bullets going through the wings. It hadn't taken me long to meet Munro's friend, the Bloody Red Baron.

Another red Albatros, this time sporting a green tail, swung in front of me, sliding sideways, it seemed, but as I lined up the gun on him, I hit his slipstream and the Pup rocked violently. By the time I had corrected the Albatros had vanished. I found him again almost immediately and fired, but the gun jammed and while I was banging away at the cocking handle, almost apoplectic with rage, I saw the green-tailed German swing round in a tight bank, and hurriedly stopped worrying about the gun and gave my full attention to keeping out of his way.

I seemed to be surrounded by Albatroses, swinging in on me like a pack of sharks closing in for the kill. Porteous and Howarth had vanished somewhere and, stuck in a tight turn, flat against the sky, the blood draining from my cheeks, I was almost choked by the thudding of my heart and furious with Porteous for landing me in this mess. The green-tailed Albatros was swinging round with me now, and I was shocked at his easy superiority.

He was clearly gaining on me, his turns so tight I could look across the intervening space into the opposite cockpit. He seemed so close I felt I could have thrown a spanner at him.

Tracers flashed past the wingtip of the Pup but I knew they were not intended to hit me, only to frighten me into changing course so that I would set myself up as a target, and I clung grimly to the tight turns. Then there was a bang in front of my nose that made me nearly jump out of the cockpit in fright as a bullet hit the altimeter and it fell apart.

Talking to myself in a nauseating fret of fear, I still somehow remained intelligent enough to do all the right things. Sykes had once told me that going into a fight was a bit like stepping into an ice-cold shower. The first shock took your breath away but after that you seemed to recover. I was beginning to recover now and it seemed to me that the only thing I could do was get down to the ground because I felt I was far too young to start dying. Flopping around at a height where the Albatroses had all the advantages seemed stupid, and I thrust the stick forward and fell out of the sky like a stone. As I did so I almost hit one of the Albatroses as it swung past in front of me. It was so close I could see its yellow spinner and the oil smears on the engine and automatically I pressed the trigger. To my surprise, because a moment before it had been jammed, the gun fired and I saw fragments fly off the Albatros and it dipped away with an abrupt jerking movement and fell out of the sky with me.

The needle of the air speed indicator was jammed against the stop now and the controls had grown stiff with the violence of the dive. Behind me I could still hear the crackle of shots and I was crouching lower and lower in the cockpit in the instinctive wish to hide myself. Made of wood and fabric, it wouldn't have helped much but my brain was almost numb with fear. The wires were screaming now and I was expecting the wings to fold back one after the other at any moment. But with the crackle of shots still behind me I daren't pull back on the stick and just had to take the chance of digging my own grave with the speed of my fall.

After a while I realized the shooting had died away and began to ease out of the dive. I had a splitting headache from the change of altitude but the Germans seemed to have gone. Lifting myself in the seat as the machine levelled off, I saw an Albatros curving away just to my right and, even as I glanced at it, it suddenly dropped through a patch of cloud, and I wondered if it were the one I'd shot at.

When I got back to Rochy, the flight-sergeant greeted me with a tremendous grin. 'Nice to see you back, sir. We heard you'd gone down like a stone, with a pack of Huns on your tail.'

'I did,' I said. 'That's *why* I'm back.'

He glanced at the machine. 'Looks like you've been through a mincing machine,' he observed.

I climbed out of the cockpit, stiff and cold and still angry with Porteous. 'What about the others?'

'Not back yet, sir.'

Howarth put in an appearance after lunch. He had crashed just behind the trenches and written off his machine, and his stricken look had intensified.

'What about Porteous?' Munro asked.

'I saw his wing come off,' he said. 'He went down like a stone near Grenay.'

That evening Latta appeared to ask if anyone had shot down an Albatros with a yellow spinner and to detail Catlow, Peckett and Bull, as the newest arrivals, as pallbearers at Porteous's funeral.

'Not what you'd call a cheerful introduction to the war,' Bull muttered.

When I went down to the hangars I was surprised to find no one working on my machine.

'Where are they all?' I demanded.

The flight-sergeant was apologetic. 'Getting ready for the cross-country run, sir.'

'Cross-country *what*?'

'Run, sir. C.O.'s orders. He's keen on physical training.'

'*Physical training!* I thought this was a technical corps and that our job was to shorten the war! Fetch 'em back here and get 'em to work.'

I went storming to Latta's office and there was a long and heated exchange. It was colossal cheek on my part – a nineteen-year-old hostilities-only officer telling a thirty-odd-year-old Regular how to run his squadron. But I was livid that two experienced technical men who ought to have been putting right the damage to my machine should be expected to go haring round the countryside in boots and braces just because Latta had a fixation about physical exercise.

It seemed to startle Latta and for a moment he said nothing, then he went for me bull-headed. But he must have known he was in the wrong because in the end, after promising several times to court martial me, he backed down and said that *my* mechanic and fitter would be excused the runs, though he made no promises for any of the others. Outside again, I leaned against the wall of the hut to cool off, horrified at the things I'd said and aware for the first time that I'd come perilously close to being kicked out of the Flying Corps or something. It seemed safer for the future to be like Brer Rabbit and 'lie low and say nuffin,' until I'd got the measure of Latta more.

The evening patrol took off already nervous after the disaster of the morning, and we were all down on the field to watch them return. Even Munro seemed a little downcast. 'Tae me,' he said, 'it seems daft tae carry the war over the German lines as we do. Sure, we're best wi' yon offensive speerit they're always talking aboot but Ah always thought that when ye were hard-pressed ye did a bit o' retreating, and consolidated until ye could hit back.'

'It makes sense,' I said.

'Oor generals were a' brought up on the Charge of the Light Brigade, though,' he growled. 'They gae bull-heided at everything. It was just the same in the trenches. Keep on hittin' 'em hard, they told us.

They didnae seem tae notice that we were sufferin'
more casualties than the Hun.'

As he finished speaking, one of the mechanics
stood up and began to walk forward, and then we
became aware of a hum in the air.

'Over to the left, sir,' the flight-sergeant said.
'Down low.'

Latta appeared and stared into the last of the
light. 'How many?' he demanded nervously.

'Two, sir,' the flight-sergeant said. 'No, three!
They're all there.'

Latta turned and headed for the office and as he
passed me I heard him say 'Thank God for that.'

As the three Pups came in over the trees, it was
obvious they'd been in a fight. Wires were trailing
and one of them bounced badly and did a ground
loop. As we all went running out to it, the pilot
jumped out of the cockpit and then we saw that
one of his tyres had been burst by a bullet. The
fabric of the machine was covered with little flags
of fabric that had flapped loose in the slipstream.

'The Bloody Red Baron?' Munro asked.

The other man gave him a wan smile. 'I saw no
Bloody Red Baron,' he said. 'But it was the same
lot all right.'

That night the farmer and his wife appeared with a small bouquet of the first spring flowers. There was a card attached to it with a ribbon – '*Felicitations au Lieutenant Falconer*' – and Munro told me they'd found out about the machine I'd shot down. It was a pathetic little tribute that left me red-faced and mumbling.

'They havenae had many tae celebrate,' Munro explained.

He set out to start a celebration but somehow it never got going and Latta's news at dinner shocked the mess. Catlow was pushed at once on to A Flight duty roster to take the place of Porteous and I was given the command. Catlow, Bull and Peckett were going to have to take their chances over the line earlier than normal, because the replacements were not coming through as fast as the casualties.

Munro was undaunted and began to pound the mess piano. '*Goodbyee*,' he sang, looking at Catlow. '*Don't cryee! Wipe the tear, baby dear, from your eyee!*'

Catlow gave him a dirty look and joined Peckett and one or two others in a gloomy game of vingt-et-un.

The next few days were quiet, however, and I wasn't sorry. It stayed bitterly cold with sleet showers and even snow and I was uncomfortable and half-frozen in a tent and not very happy. I had sent off a letter to Sykes begging him to put in a request for me, but I'd heard nothing from him and had to accept that perhaps his squadron was as busy as ours was. A couple of replacements called Winton and Smart turned up but they looked wetter behind the ears than Catlow and Bull and Peckett had been when I'd first seen them and a lot wetter than I'd been when I'd first arrived in France the previous year.

'What's it like?' one of them asked Munro.

Munro shrugged. 'Food's awful, mon,' he said gravely.

The gloom in the squadron seemed to be reflected everywhere and people were busy working out that a pilot's life wasn't more that twenty-three days. It didn't seem to me a good way to pass the time but we all knew what the trouble was. The offensive spirit that was demanded of us was in effect an offensive strategy which demanded that we should fly deep into German territory all the time, inevitably returning against the prevailing wind which blew from the west. It was the old Nelson spirit they were demanding of us, but they weren't giving us the machines to do it with.

'It's fine tae be offensive a mile over German territory,' Munro said, 'but it doesnae mak' ye more offensive tae gae *ten* miles over. No' in Pups.'

He was right, of course. Too much reliance had been placed on Government-built machines instead of allowing private manufacturers their heads. And as I'd noticed long since, those in power could see virtue only in machines so stable they could practically fly themselves. They hadn't foreseen that conditions might change and that 1917 might be different from 1915, and that what we wanted now was a machine that didn't fly itself but could do aerobatics itself and needed holding steady instead. They hadn't noticed that the old days of home-made bomb-racks and seat-of-the-pants flying had gone. Things were growing more technical and the Germans had caught on and been ready for them, and we'd been left far behind.

–

There were rumours that Latta was due to go home, and I for one was itching to see the back of him.

His obsession with physical exercise was ridiculous and he was a blusterer who could think only of reacting to the new conditions in an aggressive way that worried Bull.

'I'd have thought that doing a bunk and hanging on until we got better machines would have been much more intelligent,' he said.

'Doing a bunk as quick as poss is always the best thing tae do in an emergency,' Munro agreed solemnly.

With his future secure, Catlow could afford to regard Munro's attitude as a little unsporting. He had a typical staff officer's approach to the fighting and, if he ever made it as he hoped to the red-tab department, he had a ready-made built-in higher-command feeling. Despite his concern for his own skin, he clearly felt no one else should have any hesitation about tackling the enemy.

'Bit lily-livered to do a bunk, isn't it?' he said.

Munro grinned. 'Aye, mebbe,' he agreed. 'But, mon, mon, it does keep ye alive.'

Munro's spirits were never down for long and he was always ready to thump on the mess piano. He couldn't play for toffee but it was always possible to find him roaring out one of the mess songs – usually the most lugubrious he could think of.

> *'Tak' the cylinders oot o' ma kidneys.*
> *The connecting rod oot o' me brain.*
> *From the small o' ma back tak' the crankshaft,*
> *And assemble the engine again.'*

Somehow, however, in that squadron they never seemed to get anyone going and they *stayed* lugubrious instead of being defiant, as I'd noticed in other squadrons. The night it was announced that the Americans had entered the war, however, everyone went mad and a game of rugby was played with Catlow's cap while Munro insisted on dancing a highland fling on the table. The next morning I was awakened by soft snortings and whispered voices and found myself looking at a cow he was trying to push into my tent.

Despite Munro's efforts, however, the whole squadron was badly in need of a new spirit. The fitters and riggers hated Latta's cross-country runs because they were already working half the night to put right magneto and sparking plug troubles, and defective oil pumps, valve springs and rocker arms, and they were surly and unhelpful. Even so, we were probably luckier than many because the squadrons who'd been caught with that cursed BE, a machine which meant virtually certain death every time they took off, were having a dreadful time. In desperation they were going in for all sorts of wild ideas to improve their chances of life – machine guns attached to the undercarriages; clusters of empty bottles which screamed like bombs as they fell, to frighten anti-aircraft gunners; devices to improve contact between the crews; flares, grenades, rockets, a whole host of things which made their machines look like Christmas trees and didn't give them an hour longer of life.

They were being withdrawn at last, of course, but the changeover was slow and the RE8s, which were taking their place, were just as bad – heavy, cumbersome and sluggish – and they were being lost not in ones and twos but in fives and sixes. It had been my luck to arrive in France the first time at the height of the Fokker scare and the second time at the beginning of what was to become known as Bloody April. It was the usual trouble of too little too late, and we knew that inept politicians, some of them downright dishonest, were playing ducks and drakes with half-baked air policies, while the heads of the army and the navy quarrelled enough over aeroplanes to breed discord. Contracts were not being met and strikes at home meant that the new machines we needed were coming through only in a trickle.

'The Navy's flying good machines,' Bull said, still puzzled. 'Why can't *we* get 'em?'

'Because Winston Churchill made sure the Navy got 'em all,' Munro said.

'Can't they let us have a *few*?'

'They do, mon. The ones they dinnae want.'

By the middle of the month everyone was low in spirits. Orgill and Le Petit had grown more and more silent and Munro more noisy for the same reason. The older men were grave and worried while the youngsters, under their laughter and practical jokes, were anxious and indignant and angry with a feeling of being let down. As for me, I was neither flesh nor foul nor good red herring. I belonged nowhere, neither to the men nor to the unfledged boys. I was still young enough to long for irresponsibility, for a chance to act the fool but eighteen months of war flying had made me an experienced pilot who'd been given responsibilities and I was conscious that if I once let go, if I once started behaving with the callowness of my age, the older men who looked to me for direction might believe I knew nothing of the things they expected me to show them. I was a boy inside a man's skin. I had the undisciplined instincts of a youngster beneath the drilled instincts of an old soldier. I was mixed up, muddled, shy, and at the same time certain I must act as if I were not – as if I were as sure of myself as I was of my skill – and there were times when I felt young enough to weep and times when I felt so old I felt my feet dragged.

Of the others, Bull learned fast but Catlow, I noticed, always seemed to be suffering from 'oil pressure trouble' or a 'missing engine' and always seemed to be turning back. I knew perfectly well what was wrong. Facing the Germans in the freezing upper air was a different matter from bullying small boys at school and he was afraid. So was I, of course, and despite the fact that I didn't like him and was never likely to, I managed to feel sympathy for him. Better men than Catlow had felt the same.

By this time we were longing for the arrival of the new machines which were supposed to be coming through. New single-seater and two-seater scouts were said to be on their way which were supposed to be more than a match for anything the Germans had, but they seemed to be a long time arriving.

'Yon strikers,' Munro growled. 'Worryin' aboot a few extra bob tae spend on booze. Ah wish they'd sent 'em oot here tae tak' a chance wi' us.'

Three more men – all newcomers – failed to return, but as we entered the third week of the month Bull and Peckett were beginning to look more sure of themselves, and we even had a few small successes. Le Petit shot down an old LVG and, to his surprise, so did Bull. They found three of them wandering around the lines and, judging by their behaviour, they were newcomers and did little about taking evasive action.

Munro had moved to A Flight by this time as deputy and he and I had taken to going out late in the longer evenings looking for lost or wandering Germans. We were both old hands at the game by now and were careful not to look for trouble, and we waited as high as we could get, looking for late-flying photographic two seaters heading homewards in the rosy glow of a job well done.

Since there seemed to be little chance of joining Sykes, I'd decided to teach Munro the game I'd practised long since with *him*.

The very first night we knocked down an Aviatik. While Munro went in bull-headed from one side to keep the observer busy, I sneaked up underneath it from the other. It reared up at once as I fired then fell limply over on its side and began a long curving dive towards the darkening earth. As I leaned over to watch the stricken machine dwindling beneath me, at first I thought it was going to fall in the woods near Rochy but the steep jerking fall carried it beneath me until it finally looked as though it were going to end up in Pommier instead. Then as the arc changed once more, it moved back again towards Rochy. It was now nothing more than a moving speck against the hazy earth and had passed the woods and was moving as though it had levelled off and was heading home. Then, as it passed beyond the trees, it suddenly stopped and I saw a small speck of light glow briefly against the dusky earth.

That night Munro was noisy with delight. 'Laddie,' he said, 'this air fighting business is like golf. Once ye get the knack, it's a great sport.'

The following night, as though our luck were almost too good, we brought down two of them. The first of them was an LVG which crashed near Givenchy, sliding along on its belly, with pieces of wing and fuselage flying off, until it finally dropped into a shell-hole and stood on its nose. The second was a lonely lost Albatros two-seater which ought never to have been where it was. As we fired at it I saw a plume of leaking petrol trail out behind but the Albatros made no attempt to manoeuvre and it was still flying straight and level when I saw a red glow start under the fuselage. Black smoke followed almost at once, and a darker streamer of it trailed behind the stricken machine. Then there was a flare of flame and I saw the observer gesticulating wildly. As the flame blew back, the pilot half-lifted himself out of the cockpit, his arms across his face, his mouth open and wind-blown, and the machine, now just a mass of oil-stinking smoke from wingtip to wingtip went down in a slow curve, small burning fragments falling off to follow it down in smaller tighter curves. I had to fly through the smoke and as I came out at the other side there was a puff of flame and the machine seemed to fall to pieces, and out of the centre I saw burning pieces of wing and half the fuselage with the wheels still attached fall away. The tail section went whirring down behind and, his coat blown open as though he were trying to use it as a kite to glide to earth, the observer dropped clear. We watched him dwindle in size below us, turning over and over like a small wriggling spider until he vanished from sight.

Munro was silent as we landed and that night he got drunk. 'Ye know,' he said solemnly, 'Ah never really thought there was a man inside 'em until taenight. Ah'm no' so sure it's a guid sport after all. Yon feller was alive all the way doon.'

–

With his thick shoulders and the broad heavy head that went with his name, Bull was developing into a sound flyer. He was not skilful but he was determined and full of courage. Peckett remained what he had always been – a pale indeterminate figure – while Catlow remained just Catlow and no one was surprised when he went sick with neuralgia.

Munro made no bones about what he thought. 'Och, mon, he's scared he'll miss his staff posting,' he said. 'And neuralgia's a guid disease. No visible symptoms.'

Catlow disappeared to hospital but they sent him straight back, indifferent to his protests, and he took to mooching about alone, because even Peckett seemed sick of him.

I flew a lot of different types of machine to gain experience and, as I'd never handled one, I got permission from the FE squadron to take up one of theirs.

'Ye'll mind tae be careful, laddie,' Munro advised. 'Ah had three months flyin' yon things and if ye stand it on its nose, the engine'll fall out, and squash ye flat, like a fly.'

I took off safely but it seemed odd after flying tractors to fly a pusher again, sitting out in front with nothing between me and the sky but a little piece of plywood and the great 120-horse Beardmore engine thundering away behind. I flew it carefully. The year before I'd wrecked a DH2 trying to do tricks with it and I'd never since completely trusted that open framework that held a pusher's tail on.

When I got down Munro was thoroughly contemptuous. 'Yon's no way to fly a Fee,' he said.

'They're as tough as Old Nick's nag-nails. They'll stand anything. Watch me, laddie. Ah'll show ye.'

He took off with a great deal of flourish in a climbing turn, trying to make the FE behave as if it were a Pup. He could certainly fly it but when he was about a thousand feet up just beyond the edge of the aerodrome someone shouted in alarm.

'He's on fire,' he yelled.

Sure enough the FE was trailing smoke behind it, but Munro seemed to have caught on at exactly the same moment because the big machine banked sharply and fell out of the sky like a stone. At first we could see the flames trailing behind him and I was clenching my fists, praying he'd get down before they reached the fabric of the tail surfaces and destroyed them. But the speed of his dive appeared to put them out and as he came in they seemed to have disappeared entirely. He was still trailing a lot of smoke, however, and was taking no chances of the flames starting again and enveloping the machine. He shot across the field at full speed, bouncing as he hit the grass.

Beyond the hedge there was a vast manure heap and a duck pond covered with ducks, and he went between the trees like a rocket, tearing off twigs and leaving the wings hanging like old washing on the branches. Through the flying pieces of wood and leaves and scraps of fabric I saw a great sheet of water go up and the ducks bursting away in all directions, then there was a colossal thump and a cloud of steam, and as we rushed across the field we saw Munro heaving himself out of the wreckage of the machine in the middle of the manure heap.

'Have a crash?' someone asked with heavy sarcasm.

Munro was equal to the occasion. 'Did ye not know, mon?' he said. 'Ah always land like this.'

Apart from a wrenched ankle, he appeared to be perfectly sound, but he was covered with filth and the smell was appalling as he leaned on me.

'Can you come to the other side?' I suggested. 'It's best to keep to windward of you at the moment.'

Munro grinned, hobbling painfully on his injured legs while someone ran to fetch his walking sticks.

'Och, dinnae fash yersel',' he said cheerfully. 'Yon's naethin'. An' sure, did Ah no' put the fire oot?' He indicated the duck pond where there were a lot of feathers still floating down to the water and a few motionless white forms spread-winged on the troubled muddy surface. 'An', mon, mon,' he chuckled. 'Do ye no' see? There's duck for supper taenight.'

Chapter 5

Despite the small successes, it turned out to be a ghastly month and we lost six men in the last few days. Peckett was the first of them and when Bull was told he and Catlow and two newcomers were to carry the coffin he came into the mess with his head down between his shoulders as though ready to charge someone in his helpless rage. There seemed little hope for us because the RFC was trying to fight with machines that were slow, obsolete and useless and the end of April came in a holocaust.

The FE squadron across the field was withdrawn from daytime flying because they lost seven machines in one day and they were moved south to form a new group which was to concentrate solely on bombing Germany. None of them was looking forward to it very much but they seemed to consider it better than flopping around over the line in daylight waiting to be shot down. Then on the 28th, Latta persuaded some fool at Wing that the squadron would have a better chance if it flew squadron-sized patrols and decided that Le Petit, as the oldest member of the squadron, should lead the first with C Flight, with Orgill next with B Flight, and me in the rear with A. I didn't like it at all. It seemed to be asking for trouble.

Bull was grim faced – 'I shall bolt for home,' he said, 'after I've put in my threepenn'orth' – and Catlow made a bleated protest that he didn't feel well. But we were already too many men short and Latta insisted on him going. He went out to his machine sullenly, only too well aware that he'd been deliberately placed right in the middle of the formation so that he couldn't drift off and make his way home with 'engine trouble'.

We took off in the afternoon twelve strong – twelve drab blunt-nosed little machines moving up and down like moored dinghies in a choppy harbour. There were a lot of heavy-bellied clouds about like wet grey sails, majestic and threatening and filled with purple valleys and pinnacles. I didn't like the look of them. There were too many places for the Richthofen outfit to hide in and I didn't trust Le Petit.

As we climbed higher and higher, I caught glimpses of the earth between the clouds, the corner of a wood, a curve of the Scarpe, and once the stark ruins of Lens. I was watching for black specks against the cloud or the brief movements against the land which probably meant death. Eventually, Le Petit saw a group of seven Albatroses below and fired a Very light to draw attention to them. I was staring round the sky now, the hairs on my neck prickling – standing on end, I suppose you'd call it – and a sick hollow feeling of nervousness in the pit of my stomach as though I were waiting to start a race. I could see nothing but I knew there were Germans about somewhere. It was a sort of sixth sense I'd developed and, looking at Munro, I could see his head moving like mine was as though he were worried too.

But we were supposed to follow Le Petit down and I could see the black crosses on the machines growing in size. One of them swam out of the way of Le Petit's men right in front of me and I fired at once, and it wheeled round and fell over on its back, trailing a graceful curl of black smoke, and disappeared from sight. I felt a little better and decided that perhaps Le Petit had not made a mistake. Then out of the corner of my eye, instinctively almost, because I wasn't looking at them, I saw a whole new bunch of Albatroses coming down on us. There seemed to be about twenty or thirty of them, probably two whole *Jagdstaffeln*. Le Petit had led us into an ambush and they had sprung the trap.

It didn't seem to be the time to hang around counting and I was chiefly involved in keeping about six of them off my tail. I saw a Pup stagger across in front of me, its upper wing peeling back, then it fell away and I fired at a yellow and red Albatros but, because I had to dodge a stream of bullets from behind, I never saw what happened to it. For a minute or two the sky seemed to be full of aeroplanes, and I was ruddering frantically, my heart in my mouth, to avoid a collision. As I swung away, two Albatroses which had both been diving on me met head-on. I saw pieces of wood and metal fly off and a wheel whirr away, then the wings wrapped the two machines like shrouds as they seemed to pause, motionless in mid-air before they dropped out of sight below me. Bullets rattled and clicked against the Pup and one whined off the engine cowling so that I ducked instinctively, my heart thudding, then there was an almighty clang and the metal joystick was jerked out of my hand to whack against my knee. For a moment, I was terrified, wondering what had happened, then I realized that a bullet had hit the base of the stick and I was even more terrified, wondering how it had got there without smashing my leg. I snatched it back again and the Pup's nose lifted and, as I got my wits working again, my knee still numbed and my hand tingling from the shock, I found myself facing an Albatros head-on and saw the winking flashes from its guns and fragments leaping from my centre section. This is too much, I thought, but I kept the machine going straight and level and it was the Albatros pilot who wavered and I got a burst at him and he swung away.

The fight was scattered over an area two miles wide now, and had broken up into small circling groups, then as suddenly as it had begun it was over and I seemed to be alone in the sky. Over my shoulder I could seek a black spiral of smoke, and below me a wing was fluttering down like an autumn leaf, but there was no sign of the machine it belonged to. Two small fires burned on the ground below me.

I was still shaking when I landed at Rochy. Three machines were down already and I saw Bull's red face was a pasty purple-white.

'My God,' he kept saying. 'My God!' And he kept shuddering as though he couldn't keep still.

'Is this all?' I asked.

'Another one just coming in, sir,' the flight-sergeant said, pointing.

As I turned, I could see another Pup coming in over the trees, its motor poppling as it dropped to earth, its exhausts sending out puffs of smoke. Its wings rocked as it touched the uneven surface of the field and the mechanics swung it round towards the hangars. It looked like a sieve.

'And another,' someone called.

Another Pup was dropping out of the clouds now, its descent cautious, and I saw Latta watching it with a bleak face and anxious eyes.

'There's something wrong,' one of the mechanics said, and even as he spoke, the machine's nose dropped and it swung round in a broken sort of curve to demolish a ruined cottage at the far side of the field. There was a moment's stunned silence as the puff of dust rose into the air, then as the pilot scrambled clear I noticed a thrush singing in the apple orchard at the farm, filling the morning with its liquid song.

Bull's head was down again. 'I wonder who they get for pallbearers when the last man's killed,' he said.

There were several mechanics and fitters still waiting near the flapping Bessoneaux but no more aeroplanes came down out of the sky. Shortly afterwards, while we were still counting noses, Wing rang asking if anyone had shot down a yellow and red Albatros. I wasn't very interested because they also said Catlow had been dragged from the wreckage of his machine and sent off to hospital shot through the head and dying. The month he'd had to wait for his safe posting had proved to be just too long.

Munro turned up an hour later, with two walking sticks fashioned from a branch of a tree near a battery of heavy artillery where he'd crash-landed. His machine was a total wreck.

'How many?' was his first question.

'How many what?'

'Doon.'

'Us or them?'

'Och, who gi'es a damn aboot them? Us, laddie, us!'

I shrugged. I was still frightened and a little numbed by what had happened. In all the time I'd been flying it was the worst disaster I'd been involved in and it took a lot of absorbing at nineteen.

'Not counting you,' I said, 'five.'

'Is that all?'

'How many do you want?'

'Ah thought there'd be more. Who's gone?'

'Le Petit—'

'Ah saw him go down.'

'—Orgill, Catlow, Howarth, and Winton. And two more, including you, smashed up.'

He sighed. 'It turned oot tae be no' such a bright idea o' Latta's as it seemed, did it? Where is he?'

'In the office,' I said. 'On the telephone to Wing.'

Munro managed a wan smile. 'Ah expect he doesna' ken whether tae resign or shoot himself,' he said. 'Who're they gettin' for pallbearer duties?'

'Me, I expect,' Bull said. 'I seem to be the only new hand alive. We've only one flight left now, even if we all fly together. I wonder what they'll do with us.'

We soon learned. There were no orders for the following day and I never saw Latta again. I heard the next morning that he'd left during the night and no one was very sure where for. I was still trying to push out of my mind what had happened the previous afternoon when the Recording Officer appeared. He was an ex-infantryman with a stiff leg called Longford who was old enough to be my father. He acted as adjutant, intelligence officer and father-confessor to the squadron and his attitude to pilots of my age was mildly paternal and disapproving. I was shaving when he appeared and he waited quietly until I'd wiped my face before speaking.

'I suppose you realize,' he said, 'that with Orgill and Le Petit gone you're senior captain now.'

I didn't understand for a moment what he was getting at and the thought was enough to fill me with awe. 'I suppose I am,' I agreed.

'Well, in case it hasn't occurred to you, with the Major gone that makes you officially acting C.O.'

I jerked round to face him. 'Me?'

'Until someone turns up to replace him.'

'Good Lord!' I stared at him blank-faced. The thought of commanding the squadron – even a squadron consisting of only half a dozen pilots and the same number of battered machines – terrified me. But Longford had seen enough of the war to know just how to handle the situation.

'You know what to do, don't you?' he said.

'I suppose so. I've seen others do it.'

'Better get on with it, then, lad. There's plenty to do.'

The C.O.'s office was still the holy of holies to me and I entered it nervously. I sat down in Latta's chair, feeling that at any moment he'd pounce through the door and catch me, but Longford didn't turn a hair and simply slapped down a whole bunch of papers in front of me and suggested I wade through them. I found I knew what to do with them and it began to dawn on me that I was more experienced in administration than I'd thought.

'Does this mean I can issue orders?' I asked.

'You're acting C.O.,' Longford said.

I looked up at him, beginning to recover a little now.

'Right,' I said. 'Then the first thing we'll do is stop that damn silly cross-country running. There's plenty for the chaps to do without that.'

He looked at me gravely for a moment, then he grinned and I knew that he approved. So did the ground crews. When I went to the hangars I could see the relief on the faces there. That lunchtime an RE8 flew in, piloted by some bigwig from Wing.

'Who's the senior officer here?' he asked.

Longford jerked a hand in my direction. The bigwig, a colonel with a stiff collar and a handlebar moustache, stared at me. 'I said "senior",' he said. 'Not "junior".'

Longford's face didn't move a muscle. After eighteen months in the trenches, he wasn't afraid of bigwigs of any shape or size. He jerked a hand in my direction again. 'That's him, sir,' he said. 'Captain Falconer.'

The bigwig stared at me as though he didn't believe him. 'Are you sure?' he said.

'Quite sure?'

The bigwig looked at me. 'How old are you, Falconer?' he asked.

'Nineteen, sir,' I said.

He blinked. 'Good God,' he said. 'I see you've got the MC there. How much flying experience have you got?'

'I came out in 1915, sir. I've also done a tour of instructing at home.'

'How long have you been at your present rank?'

'Since the beginning of the month, sir.'

He blinked again and tugged at his moustache in embarrassment. 'Well,' he said eventually and his tones were more gentle now, 'I came here to make the senior captain up to major, but I hardly think you're old enough, Falconer. I'm afraid it'll have to wait. I'll have to think again.'

He obviously did. That evening, we got a message that I was to lead what was left of the squadron back to England where we would pick up a new C.O., replacements and re-serviced machines.

Munro got himself quietly drunk, almost speechless with delight. 'Praise be tae the guid God,' he said. 'Ah'm gaein' hame! Back tae Aberdeen!'

–

We flew off two days later, heading for Calais. It had taken two days to make sure three of the worst-damaged machines were in an airworthy state. The last battle had been little better than a massacre.

As we left France, a vast blanket of cloud, stretching right to the western horizon, hid England from view. Halfway across, Munro fired a green Very light as a signal of distress and began a downwards glide until he eventually disappeared as a tiny speck through the cloud below. There was nothing I could do about it except hope he was safe. I had no radio and no means of warning anyone, and all I could do was work out with a hurried mental calculation of time and speed the approximate position where he'd gone into the sea.

The rest of us landed safely at Lympne and I at once passed on my information about Munro's position. No one had heard any call for rescue, however, and we had no idea what had happened to him until the next morning, when we learned he'd spotted a motor patrol boat and slapped his machine down alongside it. A few hours later he turned up in borrowed clothes with his own in a dripping sack. Our orders were to head for Sutton's Farm near Hornchurch in Essex and Munro arrived by train and tender a few hours after we did.

The sudden transfer from the strain of offensive patrols was as good as leave and we all started planning to do a little forgetting by going home as soon as we could. But the authorities were craftier than we were. They had brought us home to regroup, reorganize and retrain after the holocaust of Bloody April, and it didn't mean we were going on leave. We weren't entitled to it, and to keep us busy they had assigned us to the air defence of London. The Germans seemed to have stopped trying any longer with their Zeppelins, but the big Gothas they'd been building to replace them were expected over the capital at any moment, so once more I found myself working up newcomers while I was on the alert to stop the Germans.

I didn't enjoy being in the office much but someone had to do the work and I was still the senior officer. We were all delighted to be in England after the disastrous month in France, however, and there were always ways and means of sneaking home, especially if it happened to be reasonably near, as mine was. Only Munro wore a lugubrious face. He didn't see much hope of getting to the north of Scotland on a week-end pass.

As soon as the machines had been checked, we were placed on a standby basis from dawn to dusk, which pretty effectively stopped any sneaking through the fence and slipping off to London, and in fact, strict instructions were given out that nobody was to leave camp. A captain called Crozier turned up as temporary commanding officer and he immediately erected a triple-horn klaxon outside one of the huts and tried a practice alarm. As the raucous screech filled the air, we were all – mechanics and pilots together – supposed to race for the machines and get them into the air. For several days we tried it until we found we could get away in double-quick time. A few replacements turned up and I thought how young they were until I remembered I was no older. Little else seemed to be done. Crozier was waiting to take command of a squadron flying the new Camels and he wasn't interested in us with our elderly Pups, and the squadron continued to bumble along in the same old inefficient way Latta had allowed.

The confinement to camp seemed a little hard but then we realized that, since the Gothas were not expected after dark, we were free in the evenings, and London was within easy reach. Despite the gloom and the lighting restrictions there, theatres, restaurants and nightclubs were still open and for unattached people like me there were also girls. I met Sykes' Cousin Charley once or twice. She gave me all the news of Sykes and, since she lived in London she also knew all the best shows.

Most of the mechanics didn't stay with us long. They were first-rate at their job and they were needed back in France where there was more urgency. We were only waiting for the arrival of the Gothas. A few new faces appeared, and then I saw one that I knew. It was Gumbell, the half-wit armourer we'd had before I'd left for France.

'Well, sir,' he said, giving me his big smile. 'Fancy seeing you again!'

'Hello, Gumbell,' I said. 'What are you doing here?'

'Just back from France, sir,' he grinned. 'Only out there two months.'

I didn't have to think too hard to guess why. Some commanding officer, driven demented by complaints about his work, had clearly decided to get rid of him. He'd probably been shunted from one squadron to another before it had finally been decided to send him home.

'What happened, Gumbell?' I asked.

'It was the C.O., sir. He shot off his own propeller.'

'He did?'

'Yessir, and *I* got the blame. He said the interrupter gear wasn't working properly.'

I made a mental note to keep a sharp eye on him.

For a long time nothing happened. We heard that the Gothas had dropped bombs on Folkestone and Sheerness but somehow the authorities had forgotten us and no one informed us until it was all over and only a few machines from training units and acceptance parks went up against them. They were hopelessly outmatched by the three moveable machine guns on the Gothas.

I kept a careful watch on Gumbell, checking my guns and filling my ammunition belts myself. The weather was improving all the time and we knew we could expect an alarm at any moment. Then Crozier announced that he had to go to Hendon about his posting and proposed to use my machine because his own was unserviceable.

I was indignant because I had taken great care with mine and had checked and re-checked it. Crozier smiled.

'*That's* why I'm taking it,' he said. 'I know it won't let me down. Take Waterford's machine. He's sick.'

I took over Waterford's Pup and inspected it disgustedly, certain it wasn't as good as mine. When I took it up I found, as I'd expected, that it hadn't been as well tuned, but there wasn't much I could do about it except put right a few obvious things then I went to join the others in deckchairs by the huts. Crozier's treachery was still rankling but the sun was warm and I began to doze. I could hear Munro trying to explain the old chestnut to Bull – 'The finest Keeng's Eenglish,' he was saying, 'is always spoken in Scotland. An' particularly in Abairrdeen.'

'And I suppose,' Bull observed sarcastically, 'that you're an expert exponent of it.'

Munro sounded surprised at the question. 'Och aye,' he said. 'An' why no'?'

I was just trying to work out who it was had first started the claim when the alarm went. As the klaxon roared I almost leapt into the air.

We climbed away south towards the Thames. Crozier had worked no plans out and we went off haphazardly. I arrived somewhere over Southend at 16,500 feet and flew along the course of the Thames. After a while I saw antiaircraft shells bursting at a point which seemed to be over the east fringe of London, and I realized there were several aeroplanes hanging in the sky there. Since they were in good formation and looked big, I had no doubt they were what I was after, and because I had taken the precaution of climbing as high as I could I had plenty of time and plenty of altitude. As the formation came past just below me I dived on the rearmost machine.

Even as I closed in I saw the bombs fall away. There seemed to be two or three large ones and several small ones. I saw them drop clear and diminish quickly in size as they headed towards the hazy blue-grey ground below, rocking slightly as they fell. As they disappeared from sight, I was closing fast on the rearmost machine. I fired at close range, but because I'd been watching the bombs fall, I'd misjudged the width of the enormous wings and I suddenly found I was far too close. I levelled off violently, almost hitting the Gotha's wingtip, holding my breath in horror and pressing back in my seat as I dragged at the stick. The swing away was so violent I thought my wings would collapse, but they held, and it was the seat-bearer that went instead and suddenly I found myself three inches lower than I had been and only just able to peer over the edge of the cockpit along the gun.

I hitched myself up with difficulty and climbed above the slower-flying Gothas again to get a good look at them. They were long slender machines with high tails and rudder and aileron extensions. They were painted a mottled grey-brown and appeared to have three sets of struts on either side, and as far as I could make out were powered by two huge motors. There seemed to be a crew of three – a pilot and two machine-gunners – though there was probably also someone else inside that vast fuselage doing the navigating through a hole in the floor.

The Germans had done what they had come for now and were swinging away in a slow flat turn towards the coast. Even as I watched they began to take up their formation again, heading east. I could see one or two spirals of smoke lifting up from the area of the river and I guessed it was where the bombs had hit, and I thought that if I could get one of the Gothas it might make up for the damage they'd done.

I dived from the right rear of the last of the huge machines. The rear gunner seemed to have difficulty lugging his gun over from the left-hand side where I'd first appeared, so, as I reached within 300 feet of him, I slipped across to the other side of him and closed in to about fifty yards and fired before he could swing his weapon across. As I curved away, flat against the air, I half expected to see the Gotha going down in a gentle curving dive, but it appeared to be perfectly all right still and I realized that the fuselage was so big I should have to put a lot of bullets into it to hit something vital.

I came down on him again from the right to swing once more over to the left before the gunner could get his gun across. I was close enough this time to see small flags of fabric lift on the fuselage and wings where the bullets had struck but still nothing happened. The pilot merely pushed his nose down a little and gained a little speed, and as I fired again the gun clacked twice then stopped.

I pulled the hammer from its restraining strap and tried to knock down the cocking handle to force the faulty round into the breech but the handle just wouldn't go down and for ten minutes I followed the Gothas while I hammered away at the gun. In the end I became so puffed I had to stop, realizing that at 16,000 feet the air was too rare for much exertion.

I was still livid with the gun and with Crozier for taking my machine, because I knew an opportunity such as I'd just been presented with wouldn't come again in a hurry, but all I could do now was give the Germans a good once-over in the hope of learning something for the next time.

I flew abreast of the rearmost machine, therefore, still within gun range, but just below and beyond his wingtip so that the gunners couldn't fire at me without hitting their own wings. It occurred to me that if Munro or Bull turned up, they'd notice that the gunners were watching me and might plunge in and knock down the Gotha while they were busy, but no one appeared and I flew alongside the German for a quarter of an hour unable to do a thing about it, and even got a few shots through my rudder from the front gunner when I allowed the Pup to slide a little forward of my position beyond the wings.

In the end over Woolwich I grew bored with staring back at the Germans so I waved and turned away. The gunners waved back cheerfully and I did a tight turn and allowed the machine to fall over on its back in a spin and dropped well below the Gothas before I pulled out and headed home.

Munro was down when I arrived. His engine had seized up.

'It was trying to run on a square ball-bearing,' he said. 'We got one of them. Did you hear?'

This was news. 'We *did*?'

'The anti-aircraft people saw one fall in a spin over Woolwich.'

'You'd better ring them back,' I said, 'and tell 'em they're mistaken. That was *me*. I was with 'em all the time and *I* didn't see any of 'em come down.'

'Did you get a shot at any of them?'

'Yes. I did. And that reminds me.'

I had seen Gumbell advancing on the Pup, his great moon smile across his face.

'GUMBELL!' For the first time in my career I managed to sound like a sergeant-major.

He came to an abrupt halt. 'Sir!'

'Are you the armourer on this machine?'

'Yessir. How did you know?'

'Because I've just been flying it, and I had to sit up there being shot at with nothing to shoot back. This is the second time you've done this to me.'

'Well, I'm sorry sir, but I'm sure it wasn't my…'

I could have strangled him. 'Gumbell,' I said slowly.

He blinked. 'Yessir?'

'Get out of my sight!'

'Yessir. Certainly, sir!'

'And damn Crozier, too,' I said as he disappeared. 'Is he back with my bus yet?'

Munro had watched the exchange with interest. 'No,' he said. 'And willnae be now. Telephone call came through. He's got his new posting.'

I was furious. 'What about my bus?' I bleated.

Munro shrugged and cocked a thumb towards the office. 'Better have it oot wi' his replacement, laddie,' he suggested. 'He's arrived.'

'That's quick!'

Munro grinned. 'He looks a quick sort o' chap. He's been asking for ye.'

I was still angry and in no mood to tangle with any cocksure new C.O. just then, and as I stalked across to the office to make out my report I was ready for anything. Longford was sitting at his desk behind the typewriter and the new C.O. was on his knees with his head in a cupboard looking for papers.

'Ah, Captain Falconer!' Longford looked up. 'Someone said there was a Pup over Woolwich having a go at the Gothas. Was it you?'

A voice came from inside the cupboard.

'Shouldn't wonder,' it said, and my jaw dropped.

'Lulu!' I shouted as Sykes turned round, grinning, and it was only hours afterwards that I realized what I'd called him.

Chapter 6

'Got home a week ago,' Sykes said. 'Went to Hathersett for a day or two to see Jane. Cracking girl.'

It didn't hurt me any more to hear him say such things and I grinned with him, delighted for them both.

He looked no different from before – bland and confident, a self-assured member of the upper classes. So upper, there wasn't a trace of snobbery or side about him. There didn't have to be. He was so upper he was almost out of sight to most people and he didn't have to do any pretending.

'How about you?' he asked. 'You got a girl yet?'

'Not yet.'

'Not even Cousin Charley?'

I smiled. 'Not even Charley. She's a nice girl...'

'—but she's not the right one.' He shrugged. 'Well,' he said, 'we always did say in the family that Charley was destined to marry a duke. Got that sort of brain. Ah, well' – he slapped my shoulder – 'have to start soon, y'know. After all, they've got you drinking and smoking – well, occasionally, anyway.

Heard you've even been bad-tempered here and there with the Hun, too.' He looked at Longford. 'Chap told me, in fact, that you manage to make 'em look so ordinary they seem to be floppin' about the sky askin' to be shot down.'

I was so pleased to see him I couldn't respond to his banter effectively, and he went on cheerfully.

'Hear you were even being nasty to 'em this morning,' he said.

'I'd have got one,' I said, 'if that fool Gumbell had done his job properly.'

His ears seemed to cock like a dog's. 'Gumbell?' he asked. 'Bad lot?'

'Not really. Just a half-wit.'

'I'll get rid of him,' he said. 'Just give me time to dig in a bit. What are they like?'

'Nasty,' I said. 'But big. Plenty to shoot at. But that means there's a lot to absorb the bullets, too, without much damage being done. What I'd give for something firing explosive shells.'

'From an aeroplane?' Longford looked startled.

'Why not?'

'It'd fall apart. From the recoil.'

I was feeling stubborn. 'You can't shoot at armour-plated aeroplanes with a popgun,' I said. 'A cannon'd blow chunks off.'

Sykes blinked. 'Good Lor',' he said. 'Aren't we nasty-tempered these days? Perhaps we could go in closer.'

'Doubt it.' I grinned. 'It's a bit warm in there. They carry at least two gunners. One at the front and one at the back.'

'What about blind spots?'

After Latta and Crozier it was wonderful to hear someone taking an interest again and asking shrewd and searching questions. 'Under the wings,' I said. 'Or behind and below the tail. And that's all. Because what the front gunner can't hit, the rear-gunner can.'

He looked thoughtful. 'Ought to do it in twos,' he suggested.

'That's what I was thinking.'

He gave me his brilliant warming smile. 'Boelcke's old dodge. Amazin' how basic it is. One to do the nasty-tempered bit and the other to guard his tail and distract the old foe. Fighters'll still be doing it that way forty years from now.' He rubbed his bony nose. 'More replacements are due in a few days and I'll be giving some of 'em to Munro to work up into a new flight. As for you, I want you to pick out a good deputy and let him run yours when you're not there.'

'Why? Where will I be?'

'With me. You and I have a date with these jolly old Gothas, remember. Dates back to last winter when we were after Zeppelins. Even to when we were flying DH2s. Must try to wreak the old vengeance.'

'I thought C.O.s weren't supposed to fly.'

He beamed. 'Blood'll run in the gutters if they try to stop *me*,' he said.

I gave the flight to Bull and told him to get it in shape. He responded magnificently and didn't hesitate to come and ask advice, though occasionally it seemed odd to me to be giving orders to a man several years older than I was.

With Sykes I worked out plans. He was involved in refitting and bringing the squadron up to scratch and he left most of them to me.

'How about firing a Very light?' I suggested. 'So that the other chap will know just when to go in.'

'Too complicated,' he said thoughtfully. 'Ought to be able to keep it simpler than that. Suggest I go in first. Offer the old body as a target, as you might say, for Hun spite. Then when they're busy with me, you nip in and shoot one of the engines out.'

'Why not let *me* go in first?'

He smiled his gentle smile. 'Can't be done, old boy. You're the expert.'

'You're a good pilot.'

'Be better if aeroplanes had reins. Besides, I couldn't hit a bull in a barn door. Better leave it to you.'

I didn't fancy Sykes setting himself up as a target, and I had sudden visions of having to face Jane with bad news as I'd once had to with her sister when my brother was killed. 'Suppose I object?' I asked.

Sykes smiled. 'Can't,' he said. 'I'm the C.O.'

So we worked it out. Sykes had no nonsense about personal scores and made his pilots practise in pairs. He gave them the choice of their partners and for the most part the teaming up was easy. Then he got down to map work and, remembering the ideas we'd discussed during the winter, he gave each pair a square of sky to patrol. This way he felt sure someone ought to stumble on a Gotha eventually.

But suddenly the Gothas seemed loathe to return. We heard of them appearing at other points of the compass but no successes were chalked up, and to cover the deficiencies of planning in the past the newspapers kept up a permanent tirade of hatred against the Germans as barbarians who killed women and children. They were careful, of course, not to mention we were doing exactly the same thing every night over Germany, but if it did nothing else it took the civilians' attention off the inefficiency of the people who had left Britain unguarded the year before with only BE12s to combat the Zeppelins.

Sykes was a good C.O., easy-going with anyone who did his job well but coming down like a ton of bricks on slackers and the inefficient, and there was a keen alert feeling in the air when he visited the hangars, yet at the same time a watchful wariness to make sure nothing went wrong. Knowing him well, it was odd to think of people being scared of him, but they were, even while they thought the world of him. The squadron seemed to pull itself up by its bootstraps overnight and eventually, to everyone's delight, Sykes announced that normal week-end leave would start again.

As I hurried off to pack my bag, he laid a hand on my arm. 'Going anywhere special?' he asked.

'Home,' I said. 'That's all. Seems ages since I saw my father and he's home, too, at the moment.'

'Bit of a family get-together at Hathersett on Sunday,' he said casually. 'Think you could manage to get away for lunch and come and see us all?'

I grinned at him. 'Nothing I'd like better: The Bartelott-Dyveton-Sykeses in their natural habitat.'

'Terrifying sight.' His face never slipped. 'I'll send a conveyance over for you.'

–

Sykes' 'conveyance' turned out to be a horse and trap driven by an elderly groom who behaved as if he were the fifth or sixth generation of his family to look after the Sykeses.

'Master Ludo says he's sorry he couldn't send the car,' he explained. 'But it's difficult to get petrol these days and he hoped you wouldn't mind the trap.'

Considering it was a spanking affair of yellow and black with brown leather cushions and highly-polished brass fittings and the day was a magnificent one, I had no objection at all to a slow clop-clop across-country. But I thought it amusing that the old man should refer to Sykes as Master Ludo, when Master Ludo wore a major's crown, a wound stripe and a pair of wings and three ribbons on his chest, and was known as a holy terror round the hangars.

The family were just returning from church when I arrived and, since they owned the living, even that was impressive. They arrived in a large charabanc drawn by two horses and there seemed to be dozens of them. Cousin Charley was among them and, whether she was aiming at a duke for a husband or not, she seemed pleased enough to see me and flung her arms round me with a yell of pleasure.

Several other cousins had arrived for the week-end too, and most of the young males seemed to be in the uniform of the Guards or one of the crack cavalry regiments, so that Sykes seemed very small fry with his wings. Most of them had ribbons of some sort and there were several wound stripes and one empty sleeve. And none of them, I noticed, wore the red tabs of the staff, as though they considered it their duty not to direct from the back but to lead from the front where the danger was.

'Always were a little weak in the head,' Sykes explained with a bland smile, as though courage were something to be slightly ashamed of.

His mother greeted me like an old friend and put up her cheek to be kissed as if I were part of the family. Jane was there, of course, and I saw her eyes were bright and happy, and then to my surprise I saw her parents too.

At the end of lunch, Sykes' father stood up with his glass in his hand. 'I have a small and very happy announcement to make,' he said. 'And that is Lulu's engagement to Jane.'

There were a lot of 'Ohs' and 'Ahs' and cries of delight and 'When's it to be's?' from the women, then everyone was crowding round Sykes and Jane, kissing them and shaking hands. Mrs Widdows was dabbing at her eyes but Sykes' mother, regal and a little vague, seemed quite unmoved, as though engagements were everyday stuff in her family.

'Of course,' she said, 'the wedding won't be for a year or two.'

'That's a long time, Mother,' Sykes objected.

'Oh, no, dear.' She shook her head. 'Not really. And Jane's still very young.'

'We're all a little young these days, Mother,' Sykes said gravely. 'We have to get what we can out of life while we're still around to grab it.'

It was a sad commentary, but our generation was one that knew no such thing as a peaceful passing away and there was a long awkward silence. Sykes' mother tried to restore the gaiety of the gathering.

'Dear,' she explained, 'she's got to have time to get used to us.'

Sykes grinned. 'Go into training, you mean?' he said.

His mother remained unperturbed. 'Well, after all, Lulu,' she pointed out, 'I suppose some people *would* call us a funny lot really. If we had any sense we'd have long since realized that we've had our day and belong really in the last century.'

She may have been vague but she was no fool, because it had long since become obvious to a lot of people that much of what they stood for had already been lost in France.

The moment, sad and a little nostalgic, passed quickly, and everyone was soon laughing again, and Charley gave me another kiss. 'Infectious, I hear, this gettin' married,' she said in the same inconsequential manner of all the Sykeses. 'Everybody's at it. If we're not careful, we'll be killed in the rush.'

I felt touched that Sykes had bothered to include me in such a personal occasion but he seemed to think it only right and proper.

'Wouldn't be the same without you,' he said. 'Besides, you had a sort of personal interest in the affair.'

The rest of the day was a hectic affair with everyone a little light-headed with happiness and all I could remember of it afterwards was a sort of rosy glow of well-being. If this was how the upper classes lived, I thought, then it suited me to be a hanger-on. Despite his concern for Jane, Sykes never forgot me, and I never felt for one moment left out of it and found myself chattering away quite happily with captains in the Grenadiers as though I'd known them all my life.

'If you survive the war, old boy,' Sykes said, 'there's quite a bit of influence around this family that might be able to help you when you go into architecture.'

I shrugged. 'I shan't be going in for architecture,' I said. 'Not now.'

He looked thoughtful for a moment. '*I'*d considered transferring,' he pointed out.

'From the cavalry?'

'Horsed charges are a bit out of fashion these days,' he pointed out. 'And gees are a bit tame after aeroplanes, don't you think? Any Tom, Dick or Harry can join a four-legged outfit. Takes an epic masculinity to go in for one with wings.'

'Will you be able to?' I asked.

'Shouldn't be difficult. There's talk of making the Flying Corps a separate service. Probably next year. The Old Man has it on good authority from a friend at the War House. There's been a commission sitting on it. To stop all the squabbling that's been going on between the army and the navy for the aeroplanes.'

'Well,' I said thoughtfully, 'they'll probably need a few chaps, won't they?'

'Eventually they'll need senior officers with ideas. You ought to make a good one.'

I'd been worrying for some time what I'd do when the war ended because there seemed no sign of it happening yet and I'd decided I was going to be rather long in the tooth to start taking examinations by then. And I'd noticed that those who'd managed to stay out of uniform were already lined up for all the best jobs. It wasn't going to be easy to find something I'd enjoy which would also pay well.

'I might join you,' I said.

–

The day was over far too soon and the following morning we were back in our uncomfortable huts and tents at Sutton's Farm. Two of the married officers had their wives in the village and I half-expected that Sykes might get Jane to come down now, but he didn't agree with wives and girl friends being around to distract men involved with the sterner business of war and she didn't appear.

The summer weather remained good but there had been surprisingly little success against the Gothas. They'd hit the Kentish coastal towns and killed over a hundred Canadian soldiers waiting to go to France, and 163 civilians in Folkstone, and had dropped bombs on London and killed a lot of children, so that the crack 56 Squadron had been brought back from France.

'What's wrong wi' us?' Munro demanded indignantly. 'Ah'm all for a fight and Ah might even pick a Blighty oot o' the raffle an' get tae Aberdeen at last.'

We continued to hope and practised quick take-offs, the off-duty flights encouraging the rest with ironic cheers as they dashed for the machines. 'Run for it, you brave lads!' they roared sarcastically, waving and saluting and flapping scarves and handkerchieves. 'Come on, you gallant fellows! Remember the women and children depend on you!'

By this time rumours were flying about that we were shortly to go back to France and we were instructed to practise tight formations. With plenty of time to waste, we became pretty good at it, the whole squadron flying together when we knew there was no likelihood of an alarm. Sykes wasn't sure it was a good idea and preferred a looser formation but some bigwig came down from London and insisted. He was probably concerned with the fact that we looked prettier that way and certainly we grew skilful at it, the three flights answering to the various signals Sykes worked out, each man with his wingtips within three feet of the next man's fuselage, and all in as tight a bunch as it was possible to be.

'Increased fire-power,' the man from London explained. 'Get in there, all firing together at a Hun formation. They'll wonder what hit them when you jump them.'

'What happens,' Sykes asked blandly, 'if *they* jump *us*?'

The bigwig didn't seem to have thought of that one, and he answered evasively. 'Fire-power,' he said. 'That's what's going to win the war. That's what's winning it in the trenches.'

'I hadn't noticed *anybody* winning *anything* in the trenches,' Sykes said to me later. 'Had you?'

He was right, of course, because the war had become a sad stalemate in France, with a daily wastage of men and no results, and the whole of northern France was being churned into a dreary wasteland of mud through which the armies couldn't have advanced at speed even if they'd wanted to.

Because the Gothas seemed to be on holiday, things remained quiet and we became very good at the formation flying, but we didn't become involved in the war again until July when the alarm went in earnest once more. The Germans, it seemed, were heading for London.

Bull and Munro were the first off with their partners, heading east and north in a group. Sykes was slow off the mark because he was occupied with dealing with Gumbell who'd been relegated to pushing a broom and couldn't even do that properly. I heard later he was let off simply because the alarm had gone. I saw Sykes running like mad for his machine, clutching his helmet and gloves and wearing an ordinary overcoat instead of his leather one, and I decided he was going to find it cold as I swung my machine round to line up with him.

We went off together, the machines waddling into position across the ground then roaring off over the end of the field in a steep climbing turn. We lifted over the houses and began to climb towards the Thames, eyes all over the sky for those elongated crosses that would show where the Gothas were. We had reached 12,000 feet when I saw them, and Sykes must have been half-frozen by then. I saw anti-aircraft shells bursting and then the Gothas just above and away to the north. Sykes waved to me and pointed and I waved back to indicate I'd seen them, too.

Continuing to climb, we headed round the stern of the formation. They had learned a few tricks since I'd last met them and were in a tight box so that it was going to be difficult to get among them. Positioned as they were, every machine was protected not only by its own gunners but by the gunners of the other machines, too, and it seemed to me we'd have to pick up a straggler or try to cut one out.

We had reached 14,000 feet by now and I could imagine Sykes feeling like a block of ice by this time. We were above the Germans now, though, and just behind them, and they looked enormous. Then I saw smoke trails in the air heading for my machine and realized they were already firing at us.

We tried our first attack on the rearmost machine as we'd planned but there were no other Pups around and we had to assume we were going to have to do the job alone. The German gunners were all wide awake and the shower of metal that came at us from all angles made us sheer off quickly. For a while, we sat above the Gothas wondering what to do next and then I noticed that they were changing course and that in doing so one of the outside machines had wandered out of formation a little as Catlow had always been in the habit of doing on a turn, and was separated from the other machines by a good 200 yards.

I fired to attract Sykes' attention and pointed, and he nodded violently to indicate he was ready. I decided to go for the German from the inside of the formation so that if he took any evading action, it would carry him further away from his friends. Sykes went in first from the outside and as the gunners began to lift their weapons round, I went down in a howling dive from the other side. Swinging up underneath the Gotha, I hung on to the propeller until the German machine seemed to fill the whole sky with an enormous black shadow. As I fired I saw pieces fly off the wings and guessed I'd done some damage but it didn't appear to be much because I saw no smoke, and every German gunner in the vicinity was shooting at me as I swung away. I saw fabric begin to flap on the wings in the slipstream and heard the crack of the bullets passing and smelled the tracer. Then Sykes was going in for a second try.

The bullets I'd put into the Gotha must have startled the pilot, however, because he'd swung even further away from his friends, as I'd hoped he would. I glanced round my machine, looking for damage, but there appeared to be nothing wrong apart from several holes along the wing, and as the gunners swung their weapons desperately towards Sykes, I went in again. Once more I saw fabric flap on the Gotha but I still didn't appear to have done any damage.

Then, as I swung away, I saw Sykes waving frantically and realized that the rear-gunner had disappeared. With the gunner downed and the huge machine drifting away from his friends, it was safe to go in directly from the rear because the front gunner couldn't reach us and we were far enough from the rest of the formation to go in together. I saw a puff of smoke from one of the great Maybach engines as Sykes fired, then I saw the propeller slow down and eventually stop.

'We've got him!' I shrieked into the wind.

I went in as Sykes swung away and saw more fragments fly off the machine. Then I noticed that one of the great ailerons was flapping loose and the machine was losing height and going down in a gentle glide, turning slightly to starboard all the time as though the pilot couldn't control it. Eventually it was heading inland again, going clean round in a descending circle, while we chased after it.

Then suddenly, while we were both firing together, the nose dropped abruptly. I was just below it at the time, pulling out of my last attack, and as the huge machine went roaring past within twenty feet of me, I saw we'd done more damage than we'd realized. The pilot was struggling to keep it in the air but he was fighting a losing battle and it was already all virtually over – so much so, in fact, we didn't even bother to shoot at it any more but simply followed it down, sitting just behind its tail.

It skimmed over a row of trees near the coast, as it continued its wide descending circle, and scraped a church spire, then I saw the chimney of a farmhouse vanish in a shower of bricks as one of the huge wheels struck it. A wingtip caught a small tree and the machine swung round; then the wheels touched the ground, and the port wings flailed the air wildly for a moment like a great bird taking a dust bath. Clods of earth and fragments of wood were thrown up, a propeller blade flew into the air in an erratic arc, and the machine cartwheeled, scattering wreckage as it went, the vast wings crumpling, and part of the tail bouncing along the ground as though it were alive, then the great machine was still.

Chapter 7

There was a tremendous celebration in the mess that night. The Gothas had had a bad day. One had been forced down in the sea with engine trouble, a second had been so badly hit by anti-aircraft fire it had had to force-land in Belgium, and the third was there for everybody to look at. Its huge rudder already decorated our mess and we had sneaked away the pilot, who was the only survivor, before the army came to take him prisoner, and filled him with whisky before sending him on his way to a prisoner-of-war camp.

There were no further attacks and it was said that the raid had been so disastrous the Gothas were abandoning daylight raids for hit-and-run attacks after dark. We felt like sitting back and resting on our laurels, and Munro even put in a plaintive application for leave, thinking that perhaps the authorities, who had already promised medals to the squadron for the victory, might take pity on him and allow him at last to get to Aberdeen.

It was Sykes who brought him the news.

'It's come through?' Munro asked. 'Ah'm gaein' tae Scotland?'

Sykes' smile was sad. 'No, Jock,' he said. 'You're not. You're going back to France. We all are. There's a bit of a fuss building up in Flanders and they want everything there is.'

Munro flung his cap furiously at the wall. 'Och, ye'd think they'd gie a chap a bit o' fun first,' he said.

The following few days were occupied with hasty packing, with a horde of local tradesmen in a panic that their bills wouldn't be paid, and a few final parties. Jane turned up unexpectedly from Fynling by train, then the following day we climbed into the cockpits, waved goodbye to the few civilian figures standing along the fringe of the field forlornly waving handkerchieves, then the Pups lifted into the air and set out for France.

Bayeffles, from where we were to operate, turned out to be a wretched place. Our equipment had not arrived and we had to sleep in tents on damp ground in borrowed blankets, and I suddenly began to feel an old man – too old for camping out in indifferent weather at any rate. There was a squadron of Camels on the field and the pilots were mad about them. They were stubby, blunt-nosed and roomy, and with a 130-horse Clerget engine and two guns they made me positively drool. The pilots said they could run rings round the Germans, who now had Albatros DVs, which were an improved version of the DIIIs that had done us so much damage in the spring. Pups, they said, were completely out-classed now so we had better start praying for Camels.

It seemed a good idea. Albert Ball had been killed in May, disappearing during a dog-fight near Annoeuillin, and as he'd shot down forty-four enemy machines by then and been flying one of the new SE5 fighters which had come out with the Camel in answer to the Albatroses, it occurred to me that if he, with his skill, could end up dead, it wouldn't be very difficult for me in an ageing Pup.

Munro's face was sad and his eyes faraway as he watched them taking off and landing. 'Mon, mon!' he said. 'Fancy an aeroplane that'll turn like a bat and climb like a lark!'

'And kill everybody who flies in it,' Bull added, trying to offer some consolation. 'I've heard they've got a nasty habit of taking off sideways and when you try to straighten out they do a sideways dive into the ground. No flowers by request.'

Thinking I might as well be ready for when we got them, I sneaked across the field whenever I could and talked to one of the Camel pilots I knew. He was a flight commander called Pack and he was clearly impressed by them, but didn't hesitate to let it be known that they weren't an aeroplane for ham-fisted beginners.

'Just take your attention off 'em for one second,' he pointed out, 'and you'll find yourself on your back or in a spin.'

'At least,' I said, 'they've built us a machine at last that isn't easy to hit.'

'It isn't easy to fly either, but you can't have everything. Take it up and try it.'

The Camel was a wicked-looking aeroplane with none of the sweet lines of the Pup, and it seemed all engine and had a curious aggressive look about it that appealed to me.

'They're tail-heavy as hell,' Pack warned. 'And so light on the controls you can throw 'em all over the sky. And just remember she swings like the blazes taking off.'

I listened to the crackling hiss as the engine warmed up then I taxied down the field. Not far away another Camel was taking off and I could see the crab-like motion I'd been warned of quite clearly. As I opened the throttle and roared across the ground, the tail well up, the engine spraying castor oil over me in a fine mist, I felt I'd never experienced such excitement in any other aeroplane before.

I was up to 3,000 feet in no time and I noticed if I relaxed the pressure on the stick for a second the tail dropped and the machine shot upwards vertically again at once. I tried a turn, closing the throttle a little because the speed seemed tremendous, but the controls became sloppy at once and I tried again, with the throttle open, and the machine hurtled round, neat, tight and secure. This was just what I'd been praying for. At last they'd built an aeroplane for fighting not joy-riding, and as I looked along the two machine guns in front I remembered the old BE2 I'd tried to fly as a fighter the previous year, with the observer able only to shoot backwards so that we'd had to fly away from an enemy in order to hit him; and the strange device I'd fixed on the first DH1 I'd flown, with a gun lashed in the front cockpit which broke loose during a fight so that I'd nearly shot myself down.

Straight flight in the Camel was much more difficult than manoeuvring but I managed to crab my way to the ground again, thinking all the time, though, that it was going to be murder flying Pups after this. As I stopped and sat listening to the click and sizzle of the cooling engine dropping spots of clear yellow oil to the grass, I saw Pack staring at the sky. There was another Camel up there, moving slowly into a turn.

'He wants to watch what he's doing,' he said. 'With Camels you end up either dead or another Albert Ball.' He squinted at the sky again and suddenly, as though he sensed what was going to happen, began to walk towards the centre of the field.

The Camel's nose dropped as he set off and it flicked into a spin. The pilot managed to pull it out but he was too late to save himself and the Camel hit the ground at a shallow angle not fifty yards away to vanish in a cloud of dust, flying pieces of aeroplane and clods of turf. People began to run but we saw the pilot scramble clear and stumble to safety, his face bloody. Pack stopped dead.

Then I noticed Gumbell not far away. We still hadn't got rid of him, and his jobs – postman, messenger and general dogsbody for the squadron – carried him all over the field. It was a job that suited him down to the ground because it enabled him to shove his long nose into everything that was going on, and he was staring now across the grass at the unhappy pilot standing by the wrecked machine dabbing at his face.

He saw me looking at him and grinned. 'That's the way to fly an aeroplane,' he observed cheerfully.

Pack gave him a bitter look. 'It's the way *not* to fly a Camel,' he said.

–

The closeness of the Camels and the sight of them taking off and pulling themselves up like lifts made us all a little heartsick. There was only one bright spot on the horizon, and that was that Richthofen was no longer around. An FE crew claimed to have shot down the pilot of an all-red Albatros and at first he'd been claimed as dead. It seemed, however, he'd only been wounded and was shortly expected back, and since he had over fifty victories to his credit now, I personally found myself hoping that his wound would keep him in hospital a long time, as his brother, who was also said to be pretty good, was in hospital, too. How the stories crossed the lines I had no idea and I could only suppose that neutral countries like Sweden and Switzerland and Holland got hold of copies of German papers which our agents there passed on.

Despite the absence of the two Richthofens, however, the Circus seemed to have lost none of its fight and was still doing a lot of damage. It was a cheerless prospect, and the battlefield seemed to match it. The army had been battering away at the German line for months now and for miles all the way to the east of Ypres the countryside stretched in a flat oasis of shell craters, each touching the next and even overlapping, and all filled with the water from the heavy rains of the summer. The only signs of life were the white dots that showed as faces turned to look up at us, but it was impossible to see the individual soldiers in their sandbagged defences – probably because their uniforms were so coated with mud they blended with the countryside. I couldn't imagine how they could even live in such a swamp, let alone fight in it. They'd been at it for months now and so far had gained a matter of about four miles with a casualty list nearly as big as the Somme.

The weather was awful with a lot of cheerless drizzling rain, and our first patrol was a disaster. Bull led four men across the lines in the tight formation we'd practised and only brought two back. One of the missing men turned up later but the other had disappeared over the German front line and had never reappeared. Bull said they'd run into a group of DVs and that what the Camel pilots had said about them was right – dead right. The Pups *were* no match for them.

The patrol that followed was also pounced on. Pups were useless at the heights at which the DVs operated and the only chance for them was to stay as high as they could, but there had been an RE8 in trouble below them and they had had to go down and take their chance. No one was killed but two machines had crash-landed near the trenches and their pilots began the long walk back to where the tender could pick them up.

'It's those tight formations,' Bull said bitterly. 'That bigwig from London didn't know what he was talking about.'

So we went back to the old loose formation which gave us more room to manoeuvre.

The first day's patrols seemed to have been an initiation because for some time after that we got off scot free and began to consider ourselves lucky. Despite the DVs, with the new Camels and the new SE5s and triplanes and a new two-seater called a Bristol Fighter, the Germans were growing less brave than they had been in April and we were slowly beginning to wrench back the initiative. We began to gain a little confidence and felt that, given some decent aircraft, we might even be able to share the excitement.

But nothing happened, though the rumours that we were getting Camels continued to multiply.

'Any day now,' Bull said.

'How do ye know, mon?' Munro demanded.

'A chap told me.'

'Which chap?'

'A chap I know in the other squadron.'

'Who told him?'

'A friend.'

'An' Ah suppose *he* was told by the cook's assistant who was told by the tender driver's mate.'

Bull became indignant. 'It's true!'

'Och, Ah'll believe it,' Munro said, 'when yon first Camel drops doon on this field.'

That night there was a lot of noise over to the east and we stood outside the mess hut staring towards the horizon. The sky was flickering with hidden flashes that lit up the trees in silhouette. You could see the light playing on the watching faces, and the whole sky seemed to thud and rumble in a way that was hard on the ears.

'Push's started,' Sykes said, standing with his hands in his pockets, his face serious.

'Hope it's a wee bit more pushy than the last one,' Munro said. 'Where's it heading?'

'Up the Menin Road, I believe.'

Munro stared at the flickering horizon. 'Ah wish the bluidy war were over,' he said suddenly in a lost lonely sort of way.

The following afternoon, orders came from Wing for an immediate squadron-sized patrol to support the infantry. The German aeroplanes were bothering them and we were supposed to go down low and clear the sky of them. I heard Sykes on the telephone, protesting bitterly.

'It's damn' silly,' he was saying. 'The last time this squadron did one of those, it had to go home to be reformed. The fighting takes place too low down for us. Pups haven't a chance at that height.'

Headquarters had made their minds up, however, and were not accepting excuses and he came out of the office frowning. 'Wish some of those fools would come up here and have a go themselves,' he said. 'Expect it was thought up by some frightful little pipsqueak who's related to the general and got a job on his staff. I'll be doing the leading.' He reached for his helmet and scarf. '*A cheval, messieurs*,' he said. 'To horse.'

'Hoots,' Munro said, without much enthusiasm. 'The mon speaks French.'

As he turned away, I stepped in front of Sykes. 'Lulu,' I said. '*You're* supposed to stay here.'

He smiled. 'Couldn't ask chaps to do what I wouldn't do myself.'

'Lulu—!'

He interrupted quickly. '*You're* going. Why shouldn't I?'

We climbed steeply eastwards, wondering what was in store. I could remember the last shambles of a squadron-size patrol, and we were all a little nervous, especially me and Bull and Munro who'd seen what had happened last time. But Sykes had been calm and untroubled and his demeanour helped to give confidence to the newcomers who were probably unnerved by our grumbling.

'As a C.O.,' he'd said cheerfully to me as we'd pulled helmets into place and fastened our buckles and belts and dragged on gloves, 'you not only have to be brave, you have to be seen to be brave.'

As we approached the lines, the anti-aircraft guns opened up on us but as usual they did no damage. Down below the whole front seemed alive, and I could see shell bursts along the whole line, the grey smoke drifting eastwards from them. Every road leading to the trenches seemed to be full of lorries or troops in column trudging doggedly east between the trees, and here and there in front of the wire we could see little groups of white faces among the mud and water as advanced parties of soldiers struggling forward through the morass stared up at us.

There was a lot of scrappy grey cloud about but no aeroplanes as we searched for half an hour in the murk for the Germans who were supposed to be worrying the infantry. The sky was as empty as the inside of a goldfish bowl, however, and I was just looking forward to going home when suddenly, in that way aeroplanes have of appearing unexpectedly from nowhere, even in a clear sky, I saw a group of dots sliding across in front of us and just above. Then I saw another group heading towards them from the opposite direction and a third climbing up to attack. Where they'd come from Heaven only knew because a moment before the sky had been a void of blue space and scattered cloudlets and now it was full of machines. Up in front it was already literally dotted with them, like a flock of starlings coming in of an evening to settle in the trees, and as we drew closer, I began to feel the old sensation of mingled fear and excitement and found myself shifting nervously in my seat to make sure I was comfortable for whatever was going to happen.

Orders had sent us over the lines far too low and we were badly placed for safety. A big fight had already started ahead of us, while above us a small group of Camels and Albatroses were swinging round and round. One of the Albatroses dropped out of the fight as we arrived below it. It had a long streamer of white vapour coming from his petrol tank and he was only fifty yards away when there was a sudden tremendous flash and the whole machine burst into a ball of fire. I saw the pilot drop clear and wondered why no one considered producing for pilots a small edition of the parachutes balloonists used. He dropped straight in front of me as the machine seemed to vanish into small pieces, leaving only a puff of smoke hanging in the air with a few fiery streaks dropping away below.

We hadn't a chance of climbing up to the scrap above so Sykes plunged with us into the main scrum. But already, the fight – as such fights always did – was attracting other formations. There were already so many aeroplanes about it must have been possible to see them from miles away, and as fast as one lot dropped out of it, their petrol exhausted, another lot joined in. Even as we reached it, I saw something flash past me that looked like a flying venetian blind and wondered what on earth it was.

Then it dawned on me it was one of the triplanes I'd heard of and for a moment I thought it was one of the new Sopwiths the Naval Air Service had got hold of. But then I saw it had crosses on it and decided it must be a captured one, until I realized it hadn't a British look about it and had the aileron extensions which seemed to be a hallmark of the Germans. I fired at it as it slipped past but it went up like a lift, leaving me standing in the slower Pup, and in no time at all our formation had broken up and we were fighting for our lives.

I saw a Pup go down, its rudder fluttering loose behind it, and another dropping like a stone with about three Germans after it, then I found I was trying to throw off about five of them. Splinters flew from the centre section struts and I saw fabric begin to flap. The windscreen flew to pieces and I thought my last moment had come as I kicked frantically at the rudder bar, skidding wildly about the air, trying to keep out of the stream of bullets and at the same time avoid collision with other aeroplanes and take snap shots at anything with crosses on that appeared in front of me. The war had suddenly become dangerous, I found myself thinking wildly. It had seemed bad enough in the days of the Fokker menace the year before but now it wasn't such a hit-and-miss affair as it had been then, with a touch of heroism about it and romantic with old-fashioned ideas about nobility and honour. It had suddenly become nasty and messy and dangerous.

I kicked hard at the rudder and fired as a triplane slid in front of me. I didn't think for a minute I'd hit him but suddenly his wings snapped back, almost as though they'd exploded and the fuselage went down like a spent rocket stick with the wings floating down behind it in great swoops like falling leaves.

I didn't have a chance to stop and stare because there were three Germans still on my tail and the Pup seemed to be falling to pieces about my ears. It was impossible to circle because there was always one of them waiting to fire at me as I came round, and the machine was in such a mess now that I knew I would never dare dive at full throttle. A wire was loose and clattering against a strut, and then the air speed indicator exploded in my face and I saw holes on either side of the dashboard and wondered how on earth they'd missed me.

It seemed to be all up with me when I saw another Pup come hurtling from nowhere between me and the Germans, and I saw it had Sykes' streamers on it. It came so close across my tail the Germans had to swerve away and I managed to escape and draw breath. As I swung round, flat against the air, I saw that they had now all fastened on to Sykes' tail, and threw the machine over in a roll to go to his help. But his dive, with the Germans following him, had carried him away from me, and I had to fight off a triplane that got in the way, and when I saw him again he was low down, well to the east of the German lines, with the three Albatroses still following him.

The fight seemed to have broken up now and the machines were scattered all over the sky in ones and twos, most of them heading for home, their petrol spent. I dropped down in a wild dive after Sykes, praying the Pup would hang together and that I'd get to him in time, but even as I watched I saw his top wing start flapping loose and he went into an uncontrolled spiral down towards a small copse of trees near Wahagnies about five miles behind the German lines. The Albatroses, certain of the victory, had drawn off and he was allowed to go down alone.

'Oh, God, Lulu,' I shouted. 'No!'

But the Pup ploughed into the trees and I saw their branches wave wildly as it disappeared and, as I roared over it, pulling out of the dive, I saw no sign of life. I swung round, wondering if I could possibly land and pick him up, but then I saw a flash of flame that seemed to reach high above the trees. The Germans had vanished now and, sick at heart and suddenly full of a sense of emptiness and futility, I turned for home.

The engine was missing badly, the machine trailing wires, the wings looking like sieves, so that I found I couldn't manoeuvre. I struggled over the trenches, indifferent to the odd bursts of fire that were directed up at me, but a knocking had developed in the engine by this time and I thought I was never going to get back. I limped into Bayeffles barely flying. Most of the Pups appeared to be down already but I was too miserable to be bothered to count them. As I turned over the end of the field the engine spluttered, coughed and died and I realized the petrol was finished and I was going to have a job to get in. But I made it, though something had happened to one of the wheels and the machine stood on its nose. For a moment I was surrounded by twanging wires and creaking woodwork and tearing fabric, then it dropped back on its tail and rocked there twice before settling.

I didn't even bother to climb out. I knew it wouldn't catch fire and just sat there in the cockpit, limp with exhaustion and misery, thinking of Jane and the way she'd looked when I'd last seen her at the engagement party.

I could feel the warm air from the engine flowing round me but there seemed to be no feeling in my arms and legs, and a mechanic's head appeared, his face anxious. 'You all right, sir?'

I nodded indifferently and began to climb slowly out of the cockpit.

'Who's missing?'

'Captain Edwards, sir. He was seen going down behind the German lines.'

'Anybody else?'

'Mr Munro, sir. And the C.O., sir. He's not back yet.'

'He won't be,' I said. 'He was killed by some pipsqueak at Wing who's related to the general.'

'Sir?'

The mechanic was staring at me, bewildered, and I waved him away and trudged to the office to make my report.

It wasn't as bad as I'd expected. Munro rang up. He'd crashed just behind the trenches and was once more making his long walk home. Edwards had crashed just behind the German line but Bull had seen him scramble clear and wave, so at least he wasn't dead. There was no news of Sykes, though

– only that stony empty silence that usually meant death.

I didn't want to talk to anyone and walked on my own across the field to get used to the idea. How long I took I don't know but when I got back, Longford said there was someone coming over from Wing to see me.

He arrived an hour later, a tired-eyed young man with wings and a string of ribbons, and I hastily revised my attitude towards the staff. This one at least hadn't got his job through influence.

'I hear Lulu's gone west,' he said, and because of the name he used I suddenly wondered if he were a relative or an old friend.

'Yes. That squadron patrol they insisted on.'

He nodded. 'None of my doing,' he said. 'I hear you're senior captain again.'

'Just,' I said. 'Edwards went down with Lulu.'

He looked unhappy. 'This is awkward,' he pointed out. 'It's the second time it's happened. You've been at the job long enough now to take the show over, of course, but they'll never give it to you.'

'Worst of being a babe in arms.'

'Yes. That's what they'll say.'

We seemed to be struggling for words. He tried again.

'They'll be sending a new chap down eventually, but for the time being you'll have to manage. Think you can run the thing for a while till he arrives? He'll be a good chap, I promise. I think Lulu deserves a good successor.'

'There were a lot of things Lulu deserved,' I said. 'But this wasn't one of them.'

'No,' he agreed. 'Well, that's the way it is. You can ask for a move, if you wish, or you can stay here under the new chap.'

I couldn't imagine Munro and Bull without someone to look after them. 'I'll stay here,' I said.

'Splendid.' His heartiness was forced, then he paused. 'I'm sorry about all this. Damned sorry. I gather you and Lulu were pretty close.'

I don't know who'd told him – Sykes, I supposed. 'That's right,' I agreed. 'We were.' Of course we were. We'd both fallen for the same girl. That always made you close, especially if the girl was Jane and the lucky man was Sykes.

When he'd gone I went into the mess. Munro had arrived. He was covered with mud after his trudge from the trenches and hadn't even bothered to take his flying boots off. His hair was still flattened by his helmet and his hands were scratched as though he'd had to scramble through barbed wire. He was knocking back a double whisky and he eyed me expressionlessly.

'Ah'm aboot tae get drunk,' he said.

I managed a smile, and accepted the cigarette he offered me with a shaking hand.

'Bad habits, laddie,' he warned, a hint of a smile appearing.

'Yes.' I nodded. 'Bad habits.'

'Ye should try getting drunk.'

I looked up at him. 'Well, I've never done it before,' I said. 'In fact, not long ago I didn't even drink. But tonight I think I'll join you. Move over.'

–

The medals they'd given us for the Gotha came through the following day but they were meaningless because nothing had been heard of Sykes and I had to face the fact that he was gone. I tried for two or three days to write to Jane, to tell her how he'd drawn the fire of the Germans who'd been trying to kill me, but somehow I didn't seem able to make sense. Eventually, Longford dropped a letter on

Sykes' desk where I was going through the reports, returns, records, the problems of replacements and repairs, and all the worries of the NCOs. It had occurred to me several times that only two years before the only thing that had concerned me was how many runs I was likely to score in a school cricket match.

I read the letter through. It was quiet, tasteful and intelligent – sympathetic and encouraging at the same time.

'It's a sort of standard thing we always write,' he explained. 'You can add anything personal you fancy.'

I delayed as long as I could and rang all the forward observation posts in the hope that something had been heard. But nothing had and the man from Wing telephoned to say nothing had been heard there either, so eventually I had to believe it, and I sat down and copied out Longford's letter and added a few limping, clumsy phrases of my own that had no hope of expressing what I felt.

Munro was in my tent when I went back to it. He looked tired and depressed.

'Yon offensive speerit the newspapers are always talkin' aboot,' he said. 'It's never mentioned by those who have tae fight.' He tapped his injured legs with his walking-sticks. 'It was all right the first time,' he said. 'Now Ah always remember how they hurt me.'

He pointed at the roof. 'It's not up there that worries me. It's doon here – afterwards – when Ah start tae shake and ma hands go dry.'

What he said was right, and I wondered what it would be like when it had all ended. All the standards by which we'd lived would be swept away then and be replaced by others of which we knew nothing. We'd be like fishes out of water.

–

The orders for the next day always came through in the evening. Wing had long since had second thoughts about squadron-sized patrols and had gone back to the normal three patrols a day and, as B Flight was on the afternoon patrol, I decided I'd be able to lead it and do the office work in the morning. I swopped with Bull and gave him A Flight.

'I'll do 'em both if you like,' he offered.

I shook my head. 'No. It's best I do the afternoon one,' I said. 'Work's the best thing.'

I was wondering what Jane had felt when she'd got my letter. I could still remember the stricken look in her sister's eyes when I'd told her about my brother and the little whimpering sounds she'd made as she'd wept.

The early patrol came back without even seeing any Germans and I reflected what an odd war it was. Sometimes you didn't see a thing, as though the whole of the enemy territory were deserted, with no one alive in it, and another time the sky was full of machines. Bull brought back the morning patrol intact, too. They'd seen a few Germans but they'd all sheered off and Bull had very wisely decided not to chase them. We all knew now that Pups were finished. They were obsolete and out of date and no match for what the Germans were bringing out, and we'd all privately decided to play safe until we got Camels.

I'd made a bad mistake swopping duties, I found, because instructions came through after lunch that the late patrol was to tackle a balloon hanging in the sky near Acheville. I knew exactly where it was and I didn't fancy the job. One or two people had had a go at it in the past but it was too well guarded by anti-aircraft guns and there were usually a few

Albatroses hanging about in the vicinity, too, in case anyone was stupid enough to try again.

We left the ground about four o'clock and flew east. There was a lot of cloud about over the German side of the line but to the west and north the sky was a steely blue colour and I could even see the Channel glittering like a belt of gold with the sun on it. Beyond it, like a faint line in the sky at what seemed to be my own level, I could just make out the grey line of England, and it was even possible to pick out the Isle of Wight. I was feeling disembodied and remote from the war, reflecting how incredible it was that I was able to sail along nearly three miles up in the air in a flimsy construction of wood and rippling fabric.

It was cold, though, the draught getting down my neck even past the scarf I wore, and the engine was running in a bad-tempered way. It had never seemed to be right since the fight when Sykes had gone and I'd stood on my nose. Testing it the day before, I'd landed with two cylinders missing but I'd thought it had been put right since. Apparently it hadn't and I was just debating whether to hand over the flight and turn home when it picked up again and, as it now seemed to be running well, I decided to chance it. It was too old, of course, worn out with the screaming strain of running too long at full throttle, as exhausted and out of date as the machine itself.

Eventually we saw the balloon, and I noted exactly where it was and flew directly at it from Acheville to get a compass bearing on it because there was a thick layer of clouds at 4,000 feet and I thought I might be able to use them. Then I turned the patrol and headed back to Acheville and climbed through the clouds and flew on the compass bearing for six minutes, deciding that it would bring me right over the balloon.

After six minutes I rocked the wings and we went down through the clouds. The balloon came up just ahead, in perfect position and directly in line. As the anti-aircraft guns opened up on us, I saw they were hauling in the balloon fast but we hurtled down on it at full speed, all of us firing at once. It looked like some hideous intestine from some prehistoric monster and I saw a lick of flame along the top of it, then it began to shrivel, wrinkling quickly as the flames ate at the fabric. A parachute opened beneath it as the observer jumped, then the crew of the lorry which contained the winch began to run for their lives as the blazing bag came down right on top of it.

We seemed to have emerged without any damage at all so we headed east again as instructed. Down below us there were a couple of aeroplanes spotting for the artillery, slow old things that seemed to be motionless in the sky. They seemed a perfect target for any marauding *Jagdstaffeln* looking for victims and I knew that normally, had they been wearing crosses instead of roundels, I would have looked them over myself. But carefully in case they were decoys.

But not today. Not tomorrow or the day afterwards. I was anxious to stay alive until the Camels arrived and I was hoping I'd see nothing.

It wasn't my lucky day. Over Villy I spotted an RE8 limping home, badgered by a group of Albatroses. It was having a bad time as far as I could see and, much as I was anxious to stay alive, I rocked my wings and pointed downwards and saw arms raised in acknowledgement.

We were going down now in a steep dive and I could see the tracers of the Germans all round the gallant old RE8, making geometric designs in the sky as they criss-crossed each other. The Germans must have been rotten shots because the old RE was still staggering along, the observer full of fight. When we arrived, they broke off at once, and the sky was filled with aeroplanes going round in circles. If it hadn't been for the RE I might have gone straight through the Germans and headed for home, but I could hardly leave him behind to hold them off alone. Despite the low height, there was nothing for it but to stay and fight it out.

It was the usual mad scramble, with aeroplanes flashing past right and left and the snaking trails of tracer across the sky. I'd picked on a red-and-green Albatros and had no difficulty in getting on his tail and I immediately felt better, certain we were going to come out of it safely to fight another day. Though I knew I couldn't hit him, I fired and, as I expected, he panicked and tried to straighten out and go the other way. I gave him another burst and the bullets seemed to go right into the cockpit where the pilot was sitting. I felt sure I must have hit something but I couldn't watch what happened because suddenly I heard the clatter of tracers flashing past my wingtips and realized I'd got one of his friends on my own tail.

I half-rolled confidently on to my back and he missed wildly and shot beneath me, a red machine with a white V on the top wing, and I was just coming out of the roll to dive after him when there was a sickening cough and splutter from the engine, and it conked clean out. It was a horrible feeling, a hideous cessation of sound, a sudden cutting of the engine's howl that seemed to hit me like a punch in the face and I immediately wondered wildly if somehow Gumbell had got at it. I knew he couldn't have but I was terrified and in the silence that was broken only by the whine of wires, I realized I could hear the scream of the other pilots' engines all round me, and the sharp crackling of their guns.

I was still hanging in my seat belts, upside down in the middle of the fight, wondering what to do, still startled, still shocked by the suddenness of it, then I dived out of the fight vertically, hoping against hope no one would follow me down and almost crying with fright and self-pity as I cursed out-of-date Pups and worn-out engines with every foul word I could find. Fortunately no one followed me and I was able to drop to safety, but we were miles behind the German lines and I knew it would require a miracle to get me home.

It never crossed my mind to think of the consequences if I didn't but I was busy, levelling out, working at the pump and the throttle, and trying to start the engine again. The propeller continued to circle slowly, but without a sign of life from the engine, and I looked down anxiously. There were columns of men moving forward but they were heading west not east and were wearing field grey not khaki, and it suddenly dawned on me what it meant.

Up ahead I could see trenches and barbed wire and drifting smoke but I knew very well I could never make it. I saw flat fields and woods and decided that if I could put the machine down there, there was a chance I wouldn't break my neck and might be able to hide among the trees and cross the lines after dark. It was a mad idea, but it seemed better than struggling on at stalling speed and dropping right into the German reserve trenches. I'd been flying long enough now to know how far I could manage to go without an engine and I knew it wasn't much further.

There was a strong smell of petrol that I didn't like at all and I decided it wasn't the worn-out engine that had conked after all but a feed pipe that had come adrift somehow. I knew I hadn't been hit. I'd only been in the fight for a matter of a few seconds and none of the bullets that the following German had fired at me had come anywhere near me.

My flying boot was wet with petrol now and I could even feel it chilly through the sheepskin, and I prayed I could get down without bursting into flames. I found a big field near a wood and, as I turned over the end of it, I found myself wondering what Jane would feel, because she could hardly yet have got over the news about Sykes.

By this time I was almost stalling and I dropped the nose then pulled back the stick and, as I felt the rumble of the wheels on the ground, I let the machine roll on until it was almost alongside the wood. I still had ideas of bolting into the trees but, even as the machine stopped and I jumped to the ground, I realized that I wasn't going to be that lucky. I could see a German on a horse galloping across the field towards me, followed by several men on foot carrying rifles. I had no idea where they'd come from and could only imagine they were part of one of the regiments moving to the front and they'd seen me come down.

I didn't have to worry about turning on any taps to let the petrol flow. All I had to do was grab the Very pistol and aim it into the cockpit. The machine went up with a 'woof' that blew me back off the wing and singed my eyebrows, and I landed flat on my back with all the breath knocked out of my body. When I recovered my wits, I was looking up at the man on the horse who was pointing a revolver at me.

'You are my prisoner,' he said in English.

Chapter 8

As I climbed slowly to my feet, numbed and sick at heart at the idea of captivity, a big Mercedes tender came hurtling through the open gate of the field and bounced across the grass towards us. As it skidded to a stop that sent the back end round in a half circle, another officer jumped out and advanced towards me.

'You are my prisoner,' he said, also in English.

I indicated the man on the horse. '*He says*,' I pointed out, '*that I'm his.*'

He turned and stared at the man on the horse, then he launched into a tirade of German that I didn't understand. A noisy argument developed while the men with rifles stood looking on, gaping, and the driver of the Mercedes watched with a grin on his face. Finally, with a final bark of annoyance, the man on the horse put his revolver away and snatched at his horse's head. The man who'd been arguing with him turned to me and smiled. 'We have settled that,' he said. 'You are *my* prisoner.'

'I'm glad you've sorted it out,' I said. 'You speak very good English.'

'May I present myself? Leutnant Krefft. Hermann Krefft. I went to school in England. My father married an English woman. She died and we returned to Germany. If my father had died, I would probably have been fighting with you instead of against you.'

The man on the horse had his men in formation now and was marching them away, his face showing his disgust. Krefft smiled.

'We cannot let fliers go into some wretched infantry prison,' he said. 'Not after we take the trouble to shoot them down.'

For the first time I felt I was one up on him. 'You didn't shoot *me* down,' I said.

'Not I myself,' he said. 'My squadron. I was watching.'

'Not even your squadron,' I said. 'It was just an old worn-out engine. It conked. It was getting no petrol.'

'Ach, so!' He smiled again and glanced at the burning machine. Like all petrol blazes, it was dying quickly but there wasn't much left of the Pup. The fuselage had sagged and the engine had dropped out of the housing and there was now little more than a sooty smell in the air and a drifting cloud of oily smoke. 'Never mind,' he said. 'We will still do you the honour of entertaining you. Have you many victories?'

'One or two.'

'Our leader has many. Sixty-one, in fact. You will perhaps have heard of him. Baron von Richthofen.'

I'd heard of him all right. I'd had bad dreams about him often.

Krefft was holding the door of the Mercedes open. 'Tomorrow, unhappily, you will have to go to prison just the same,' he said. 'But for tonight we shall be able to make the thought of it more acceptable.'

It was an odd feeling to be driven along a row of mixed Albatroses and triplanes in front of canvas hangars that billowed and fell in the gusty wind that was getting up. It seemed strange to see them so near with empty cockpits, and faintly unnerving to think I'd sometimes had to sit in front of them while they fired at me. Most of them were red with ailerons or tail surfaces painted in other colours and as we passed in front of an all-red triplane, Krefft gestured.

'Richthofen's,' he pointed out. 'Doubtless you've seen him in the air.'

'Not in that,' I said.

'Then he would be flying an Albatros. He prefers the Albatros.'

I was eyeing the aeroplanes with interest, noticing just where they stood in relation to the rest of the airfield. Krefft smiled. 'I expect you are wondering whether you could steal one,' he said. 'I assure you, you could not.'

It was strange to be ushered into a mess where the trophies on the walls were red, white and blue roundels instead of black crosses and I recognized at least one number as one of ours. There was that strange stale smell that came from the cigars the Germans always smoked, and I noticed that over the bar there were photographs of smiling young men in uniform who Krefft said were former members of the squadron who'd been killed. It seemed a funny way to decorate a bar.

There were three officers standing nearby, two of them still wearing leather coats, and they clicked their heels as Krefft introduced us.

'Hauptmann Falconer,' he said. 'Leutnants Von der Osten, Pastor and Gontermann. The

Rittmeister will be back shortly, when he has chased your friends from the sky. What a pity you weren't here yesterday. Then you might have met Leutnant Voss. You have heard of Werner Voss.'

I hadn't and he told me his score was almost as high as Richthofen's.

Someone put a glass of cold wine into my hand and someone else helped me off with my leather coat, and a third offered me a cigar, which I allowed them to light for show and then allowed to go out because it was far too strong for me. After a while I heard the motors of returning aeroplanes and heard them dropping overhead to land.

After a while a car drew up outside with a squeak of brakes and the door opened. Immediately everyone clicked to attention. The man who came in was small and blond and wore a cross at his throat. Krefft saw me looking at it. 'The *Pour le Mérite*,' he said. 'It is the highest award we can give a soldier. It is equivalent to your Victoria Cross. We call it the Blue Max because of its ribbon.'

I was watching Richthofen with interest. He seemed older than I'd expected and looked tired and lacking in enthusiasm.

'How old is he?' I whispered to Krefft.

'Twenty-six,' he said.

'He looks older.'

He glanced at me. 'How old are you, Herr Hauptmann?' he asked.

'Nineteen.'

He gave me a grave smile. '*You* look twenty-six,' he said. 'It is the war.'

As Richthofen approached us, Krefft came to attention. 'Herr Rittmeister,' he said. 'May I present Hauptmann Falconer?'

Richthofen lifted his eyes to mine. He seemed a rather reserved grave young man who had grown old too quickly. He touched my medal ribbons and said something to Krefft who translated for me.

'The Rittmeister says he is pleased to see you are an honourable flier,' he explained, 'and he hopes you will be able to eat with us before the provost people come to remove you to prison.'

I woke up the following morning with an awful hangover. I had indeed eaten with them, and I'd drunk with them, too. It seemed to be their pleasure to get me drunk – not, I felt sure, to make me feel stupid, but just to make the thought of prison a little easier.

Krefft was standing over me, smoking. 'I regret to say,' he said, 'that there is a car waiting outside. It will take you to town until the authorities can move you further into Germany.'

I couldn't feel anything for him but friendship, because he and his comrades had not only spared my life but they had spared my pride, too. They had made no gestures of anger or reproach and had only shown a ready sympathy with my plight, linked with me in what we felt was a fraternity of the air. After the first stiffness and formality I had even managed to enjoy myself, though it didn't alter the fact that someone – and I'm sure it wasn't one of the pilots – had been through the pockets of my coat while I was eating and removed my money.

He paused while I washed. 'We have had bad news today,' he said.

I looked round. 'Oh? What's happened? Have *we* won the war?'

He managed a stiff smile. 'No. We have heard that Voss has been killed. He was caught last night by several of your new fighters and was shot down near Poelcapelle.'

I remembered how he had spoken of Voss the previous day and I said I was sorry.

He shrugged and offered me a couple of battered books. To my surprise they were Jane Austen's *Pride and Prejudice* and Thackeray's *Vanity Fair*.

'Old student books of mine,' he explained. 'I used them to keep my English sound. Perhaps they will help the – the' – he hesitated – '*die furchtbare Langeweile* – the frightful boredom of captivity.'

The words were as bad as a blow in the face. Up to that point, with the entertainment they'd offered me, I had hardly thought much about captivity but now it was brought home very forcibly.

The driver of the Mercedes drove as though all the devils in hell were after us and the bounces made my head rattle inside as though something were loose. The wind was blowing flurries of rain against the windscreen and I could see the trees bending under the growing gale. Mercifully I fell asleep and stayed that way until the car pulled up with a jerk in what appeared to be a small town.

A red-faced German with a spiked helmet barked at me as I climbed out. He didn't salute me, though the driver of the Mercedes did. As the car drew away, I was led inside what appeared to be the headquarters of a German military police unit and the man in the helmet handed me over to another German. I guessed he was the town provost officer because he looked too old and too fat to be part of any fighting unit.

He began barking questions at me at once in a mixture of English and German but I gave him only my name, rank and number as I had to, and nothing else. I wasn't offered a chair and had to stand there stoically, aware only of an aching head from which I felt everything would spill out if I bent too far forward, and simply repeat my name, rank and number to every question he barked at me. When I didn't co-operate, he grew angry and began threatening me. I didn't understand much of what he said when he spoke in German but I did understand '*Sofort totgeschossen*' – 'shot dead at once' – and I guessed what he was threatening me with if I tried to escape.

'Never will you do it,' he said. 'It is not possible. *Über die Gräben gehen ist nicht möglich.*'

He was telling me that it was impossible to get across the trenches and I didn't argue with him because I guessed he was right.

After a while, he grew tired of insulting me and barked something to a sergeant who touched my arm and indicated a door. Beyond it I saw stairs. I was in what I supposed was the clearance station for captured officers on their way further into German territory. On the next floor a door was opened and I stepped inside. There were two iron bedsteads in the room beyond, both covered by straw-filled sacking mattresses, but there seemed to be only one shabby-looking blanket and under it a man was sleeping face-down. As I appeared, he stirred. I crossed to the other bed and sat down, filled with gloom. The increasing wind was clattering a shutter somewhere and the walls were covered with peeling whitewash on which a few people who had been in there before me had written their names. There were none I knew, but in one corner were the words, 'Abandon hope all ye who enter here' and it summed up my mood exactly. The grey white peeling walls sent my spirit sinking to my boots. This was what it meant to be a prisoner, and I felt bitterly angry – not at anyone in particular but at the unkindness of the fate that had chosen me. At nineteen, life seemed urgent and there seemed a great need to hurry, and the idea of spending

months, years perhaps, in prison was a grey suffo-
cating thought that left the future empty of hope.

Then I realized that the man on the other bed
was sitting up. Slowly he turned to face me.

'Good Lor', Brat,' he said. 'What are *you* doing
here?'

–

Sykes hadn't changed a scrap – airy, indifferent,
casual, scruffy for once and even, it seemed, a little
batty and bored, but bursting with self-confidence.

'How long have you been here?' I asked.

'Few days now,' he said. 'Did a sort of flat spin
into the ground and stepped out of the machine just
as it went up in flames. Not a scratch. Amazin'.' He
beamed at me and I wished my headache wasn't
so bad, so I could enjoy the occasion more. 'Bolted
for the trees and hid there. Rather hoped I'd be able
to nip home. Didn't work, though. Ate things like
turnips and potatoes from the fields for a couple of
weeks. Got a bit hungry in the end. But they knew I
wasn't dead. No body, y'see, and they were looking
for me all the time. Suppose they're waiting to send
me off to the old dungeons now. How about you?'

'Those blasted Pups!' I said bitterly. 'I conked in the middle of a fight. I spent last night dining with Richthofen.'

'What's he like?'

'He looks tired. Like Munro.'

I looked round the bleak little room. It was about fourteen feet square, with bare walls and bare boards, and two small windows with leaded lights set high in the wall out of reach and separated by a slender stone mullion.

'What's it like in here?' I asked.

'Grub's not so good. And there's only one blanket.'

'We'll have to take turns with it,' I suggested and he looked shocked.

He rubbed his bony nose and offered me a cigarette from a crushed packet. 'German,' he pointed out. 'One of the guards gave them to me. Smiled at him like a Dutch uncle and he seemed to feel guilty and pressed them into my hand.'

I wasn't surprised. He had enough charm to cajole the Devil himself.

For a long time we sat in silence, then I looked up. 'I can't stay here,' I said. 'I'll go sprat-eyed in a prison camp.'

'Got any plans?'

I shook my head. 'Where are we?' I asked.

'Lambres. Near Roubaix.'

'How far from the trenches?'

'Twenty kilometres. Ten to fifteen miles.'

'It's not far to walk.'

He smiled. 'Forgotten the old battle,' he pointed out. 'Front'll be teeming with troops. Much better to head for the coast and pinch a boat.'

'Well, we'll worry about that when we're out of here. Got any ideas?'

'A few.' He indicated the window. It was set in a deep recess, higher up than we could reach.

'We can't get up there,' I said.

'Yes, we can,' he said. 'I've been.' He gestured at the two iron-framed beds. 'Put one of those on top of the other. Like a ladder. Took the old boots off. Hard on the toes, but you can do it.'

I looked up at the window. 'Isn't it locked?' I asked.

'No.'

'*It isn't?*'

'No.'

'That makes it easy.'

'Not all *that* easy.'

'Why not?'

He grinned. 'It's nailed.'

I could have hit him with the bed. 'That's that then,' I said.

'No, it isn't.' He was still cheerful. 'The Germans obviously never had to nip in home after the Old Man was in bed.'

'Did you?'

'Often as a boy. Went poaching. Father's pheasants. Chap in Hathersett used to take me and show me what to do. Always thought it rather funny, me pinching my own father's pheasants.'

'What's that got to do with the window?'

'He'd once done a bit of burgling in his spare time. Showed me how to get in when I got home. Leaded lights, y'see. All you need is a penknife.'

He fished in his pocket and produced a spoon. 'Swiped it,' he said. 'When they weren't looking. I've been rubbing it against the stone there ever since I arrived.' He indicated a square of flinty stone showing through the whitewash, and I saw there was a long mark on it. 'Got quite a point on it now.'

I stared at him in admiration. 'Are you sure *you've* not done time for burglary?'

He grinned and I looked up at the window again. 'What's on the other side?' I asked.

'A roof.'

'Far down?'

'Twenty feet.'

'We can't drop that far,' I said. 'We'll go clean through it. The row'll be enough to wake the dead.'

'Not really, old boy. How long's the choker you're wearing?'

I stared down at the scarf Jane had knitted for me, and then for the first time I saw that he was wearing one, too. I'd seen it before but I'd never really noticed it.

'Jolly near seven feet, I should think,' I said. 'Jane knitted it. I asked for a good long one to keep the draught out. How long's yours?'

'Seven feet.'

'Same as mine.'

'Didn't have to tell her the length. She knew it.'

He grinned and I realized that Jane had knitted that one, too, after she'd shifted her allegiance.

'What's in your mind?' I asked.

'Tie 'em together,' he said. 'Gives us around twelve feet, give or take a bit. More if we tie 'em to the blanket and the blanket to the mullion there. Should be enough to get us down to the roof.'

'Are they strong enough?'

'Jane was a good knitter.'

I grinned. 'Good old Jane. When?'

He blinked. 'Tonight?'

—

We waited until the place was dark and, although my watch had been broken and Sykes' had been stolen by the men who'd captured him, we guessed it was somewhere in the early hours of the morning. The wind had grown stronger and the loose shutter I'd heard was clattering constantly.

'You awake?' Sykes said.

'I've never been asleep.'

'Let's get going. I'll put the glass in my pocket.'

Carefully, moving slowly so as not to make a sound, we stripped the two beds of the mattresses and placed one of them against the wall. Then we stood the other one on end on top of it, its legs to the wall, and knotted the two scarves together and tied them to the solitary blanket.

'Ready?'

'Yes.'

He wrenched off his boots and, while I steadied the beds, he dug his toes into the angles of the bedsprings and made it to the top. He had to wriggle over the bar at the head of the bed to get to the recess where the window was but he made it and I could see him levering away with his sharpened spoon at the lead that held the glass. After a while I felt a draught on my face and saw he had removed several panes and was sawing at the lead. He had soon made a hole over two feet square in one window and a smaller one in the other.

'Chuck us the blanket end.'

I handed it up to him and he knotted it round the mullion through the openings he had cut, then he pushed the scarves and what was left of the blanket outside.

'Ready?'

'Yes.'

'Shove my boots up.'

I handed them up to him and he glanced outside. 'Better come up now,' he said. 'I'm going out.'

I saw him struggle through the window to the ledge outside, then I took off my flying boots and began to scramble up the bed after him. Half-way up, the lower bed moved with a scrape along the floor and, thinking the whole lot was going to come crashing down, I made a quick grab at the mullion and hauled myself up. It was an awful job getting over the bed-head and the hole didn't seem big enough for me with my boots tied round my neck, and outside the wind hit me like a blast and nearly unbalanced me. A whisper came up from the shadows below.

'Where've you been, you ass?'

I didn't bother to reply and lowered myself down. The blanket and Jane's scarves did their job well and I felt Sykes' hands guiding my feet to the ridge of the roof. They slipped at first and a tile was dislodged and went sliding down the roof to the guttering with a clatter. We crouched against the wall, holding our breath, but the wind was rattling the shutter again and there was no indication that anyone had heard.

'Where do we go now?' I asked.

'Haven't the faintest,' he said. 'Haven't been out before.'

Plucked at by the gale, we edged down the roof and along the guttering. There was another small roof sloping away just below at the end that we hadn't seen, and we lowered ourselves to it and slithered down to the next guttering. It brought us another ten feet nearer the earth. Fortunately the wind hid all the little scrapings and slitherings we made.

'How far up are we now?' I said.

We peered cautiously over the edge. The clouds had covered the moon and it was hard to see in the darkness but we still seemed to be pretty high off the ground. We were looking down on a stableyard and Sykes smiled.

'Over the dungheap,' he said.

I remembered as a child at the Widdow's farm jumping off the roof into the spongy pile beneath and grinned. It had been soft and had absorbed the shock. Below us was a small walled enclosure filled with the soiled straw.

'Anything's better than sitting about like a sack of wet spuds,' I said.

'Not half,' Sykes murmured and before I knew what had happened he'd gone.

I was just going to jump after him when I realized my boots were still round my neck and I sat on the edge of the guttering to drag them on. It was surprisingly difficult on the steeply sloping roof and once I almost lost one of them.

'For heaven's sake!' I heard Sykes' whisper float up from below. 'Come *on!*'

I got the boots on at last and jumped. As I landed I fell sideways and cannoned into Sykes. We both fell against the wall, and as we lay there, I heard a door open and a voice say something in German. I was over the wall in a flash and diving for the shadows. The door closed again and I was able to creep along the side of the stable to the open gateway. Outside there were some bushes and I dived behind them in a panic of fear.

I'd lost Sykes and stared around in the dark, frantic.

'Lulu,' I hissed.

'Here, old boy!' The voice came calmly from alongside me and made me almost jump out of my skin.

'You *sure* you've not done time as a burglar?' I said.

'Three years. Hard labour.'

He began to mutter and seemed to be feeling his rear.

'What's wrong?'

'The glass,' he said.

'What's wrong with it?'

'Sat on it. Cut the old behind, shouldn't wonder.'

The wind was still rattling the shutters above us and making a roaring sound through the trees, and somewhere in the building, where I imagined the guardroom was, I could hear a piano and a man's voice.

We got our bearing from the stars and set off westwards out of the town, moving along the walls in the darkness, but as we turned the corner, we were horrified to see a group of soldiers lounging under a light in an open gateway in front of us. It looked like the entrance to a warehouse they were using as billets. We froze into the shadows, but just at that moment, a man appeared from a doorway just inside the gate, and started shouting and the men hustled into a group. There were more orders, and they sloped arms and began to march off down the street in the direction we'd intended taking. After a while, we heard more shouting, and the clatter of rifles, then we saw matches flare and realized they'd been halted again and allowed to fall out – right across our path.

'That's torn it,' I said.

'Have to try a different way,' Sykes said, and melted into the shadows again so that I almost lost him.

He'd turned down an alley and was glancing up at the stars. 'Heads north,' he said. 'If we walk far enough, we can reach the coast. All we have to do then is swim the Channel.'

We were soon in the open countryside, where we could hear the thudding of guns to the west. After a while I began to grow hungry and could feel a blister on my foot. I realized that flying boots were never made for marching in but I struggled on as the pain grew worse.

'Lulu,' I said. 'I've got a blister.'

'Me, too,' he said cheerfully. 'Two. One on each foot.'

I felt ashamed of my complaint but felt sure my blister was bigger than both of his put together. Sullenly, I tramped on, always a step or to behind him. There wasn't much of Sykes. He was so slender we always used to say that if he turned sideways he became invisible, but he had an immense store of whipcord strength, and his pace never seemed to slacken. We must have put twenty or thirty kilometres behind us before we began to see the first streaks of dawn.

'Better hide for the day,' Sykes said.

'Good,' I said. 'I've got *two* blisters now.'

'Funny how they multiply,' he said. '*I've got four!*'

I felt like hitting him over the head for his cheerful optimism and indifference to discomfort, but I knew it was all put on for my benefit. He came from a family which had always produced leaders and it was his job to lead – and leading didn't just mean walking in front.

We found a big barn just as it began to grow light. It was part of a group of buildings that seemed to be attached to a country house – as though the owners had been wealthy farmers of some sort. But the place looked deserted and we decided that, because of its nearness to the front, they had long since vanished.

'This'll do,' Sykes said.

We crept into the barn which was full of straw and felt warm after the cool of the autumn night. I flung myself down and began to wrench off my flying boots. To my surprise Sykes seemed to have fallen asleep already. He'd covered himself with straw and disappeared from sight. I did the same and lay back.

I was asleep within seconds.

–

I came to life with a jerk, certain I was being attacked. I'd heard a yell of anger and as I sat up, scattering straw, I saw Sykes emerging also, his face a picture of indignation. In front of him, holding a pitchfork, her face as startled as mine, was a girl. She was about eighteen and pretty in a dark foreign way and, though her clothes looked good, I noticed she wore wooden clogs on her feet and a heavy apron.

'*Messieurs,*' she whispered. '*Vous êtes anglais?*'

Sykes was rubbing his rear but he recovered his composure sufficiently now to answer her. '*Oui, Mademoiselle,*' he said. '*Pilotes anglais.*' He turned to glance at his trousers. 'Spiked the old behind,' he muttered. 'Same place the glass got me.'

'*Monsieur, excusez-moi, s'il vous plait. Je ne*' – the girl halted and blushed and fought to find the words in English – 'I do not know you are here.'

Sykes was on his feet already, being gallant. I was being what I considered more practical and was looking for an escape route, but I hadn't reckoned with Sykes' charm. He was chattering away now in French, only parts of which I could grasp with my limited knowledge of the language, and the girl was answering him. She looked frightened but then I saw her give a little smile.

She jammed the pitchfork into the straw and turned away. Sykes turned to me as she vanished through the door.

'Where did you learn to speak French like that?' I asked.

'French governess, of course,' he said. 'All the best people have one. Didn't you?'

'My mother brought *me* up.'

He shrugged. 'Expect that's why you've got that nasty realistic attitude to life. Makes for bad temper.' He scratched gently.

'Fleas?' I asked.

He nodded. 'Light infantry. Skirmishing all over me.' He glanced at his behind. The pitchfork had torn a hole in his breeches.

'Much damage?' I asked.

'Fearful. In need of a tailor.'

I glanced at the door, not at all sure that light-hearted banter was the right approach to escape. As

Sykes said, I had a realistic attitude to life. 'Suppose she goes to fetch the Germans,' I said.

'No self-respecting Belgian would help the people who'd trampled all over her country.'

'Suppose she's not self-respecting? Just frightened.'

I was all for bolting but Sykes was quite confident, though he almost had to sit on me to make me stay. I was twice as surprised, therefore, when the girl returned with a long French loaf and a jug of milk.

As she sat and watched us eat, we asked her questions. It appeared we were just outside a village called Noyelles and it seemed her family had business interests in Ghent. They had manufactured sewing machines there and this was their country home, and because the Germans had taken over the business and were now using it to make machinery for the German army, they had all been forced to live there. Her father spent most of his time in Tournai where the Germans had allowed him to set up a small factory to manufacture for the German market, but he rarely visited the farm these days and with the farm workers all gone, the work had to be done by herself and her mother.

'But now we have only two cows and one horse,' she said. 'So there is not a great deal to do.'

She didn't speak English like someone who'd spent all her life working on farms and when I questioned her more closely it appeared she'd had to leave school because the building had been destroyed by shelling in the first days of the war. She looked intelligent and gentle but she seemed to suffer from no bitterness about what had happened.

'The war will end soon,' she said, 'and we shall return to Ghent.' She smiled and gestured at us. '*You* will make the war to end.'

To me, the war looked like going on for ever, but Sykes was much more of an opportunist.

'Not while we're *here*,' he explained.

She seemed to catch the point at once, and we picked her brain on the possibility of escape for the next half-hour. But she'd spent the last three years on the farm and didn't know much of what was going on beyond its boundaries. While we were still talking, I heard a door slam outside and a voice call.

'Marie-Ange!'

'*Ici, Maman.*' The girl turned her head and called. '*Je viens tout de suite!*' She scrambled to her feet. 'It is my mother. I must go. She will not come here. She is not well and stays by the house.'

As she disappeared, Sykes burrowed back into the straw.

'Cracking girl,' he said.

–

The girl returned about an hour later, this time with slices of meat wrapped in a red and white serviette, and two or three tomatoes. It turned out that her name was Marie-Ange de Camaerts, and she had visited England as a child to see the coronation of George V with her parents and had never forgotten it.

'All was so beautiful,' she said ecstatically, her eyes lighting up for the first time, so that the wary uneasiness vanished. It transformed her. She had the sort of face that was solemn in repose but the smile completely changed it. Doubtless she'd been driven deep into her reserved nature by the war and the arrival of the Germans. Her adolescence had been a time of oppression, fear and anxiety, but it was obvious a much livelier individual was there beneath the shy exterior.

We began to talk of the possibilities of escape again, and she promised to help.

'I will take you to Middelkerke,' she promised. 'You can perhaps then steal a boat and go to Dunkerque. I have relatives who have a house at Wilskerke where you can hide. I will go into Tournai and obtain a permit to visit them.'

'How will we get to Middelkerke?' Sykes asked.

'We must walk. It will occupy two or three nights.'

'It must be a hundred kilometres,' I said. Thinking about my blisters, the idea shocked me.

She looked at me, her head on one side. 'So?' she said.

'That's a long way.'

'I think perhaps,' she said, 'that you do not wish to escape enough.'

Chapter 9

We spent the next days listening to the rumble of battle to the west and arguing fiercely over the merits and demerits of travelling in the dark or by daylight.

Marie-Ange arrived in the barn from time to time to bring food – once a feast of cooked lamb chops and fried potatoes with a bottle of wine.

She was excited. 'I have to get the permit,' she said. 'It is not easy. They do not like us to move about. But I smile a lot and they give it to me.'

She looked at me gravely, small and fragile, and I realized that under her solemn exterior there was no shortage of will.

'When do we go?' I asked.

'You are in a hurry?' she said.

'No, no,' I pointed out quickly. 'But while we're here you are in danger.'

'I have been here for three years wanting to do something for my country,' she said. 'Now I do it.'

Later that day, her mother appeared in the barn, small like Marie-Ange but with the same grave manner and leaning on a stick. She accepted our greetings like a great lady and oddly she reminded me of Sykes' mother. The De Camaerts, it appeared, were a wealthy family by Belgian standards and they were being forced to live under much harsher conditions than they had ever been used to. She said she had books in the house which we might like to read – English books which they'd had in Ghent – and Sykes offered to help her find them. Marie-Ange stayed in the barn with me and as Sykes disappeared we both became silent. The thud of the guns came plainly over the fields on the wind.

After a while she looked at me. 'When you arrive,' she said, 'you do not trust me, do you?'

'Of course I do!'

'I do not think so. I see your face. It is much worried and you are anxious to go.'

She had keener eyes than I'd realized. 'Well, I'm not now, Marie-Ange,' I said stoutly. 'I think – I – well, I think you're pretty hot stuff.'

'Hot stuff!' She frowned. 'What is "hot stuff"? Something to eat?'

I grinned. 'No. It's slang. *Argot*. It means – well, it means you're awfully good – and awfully pretty, too! We use it about our aeroplanes or anything we think is pretty good.'

She stared at me gravely for a moment, then she smiled slowly. I'd already decided that the moments when she smiled were the highlights of the day in the barn.

'The English are very funny,' she said. 'When something is good you say it is awfully pretty and when it is bad you say it is pretty awful. It is very difficult to understand.'

–

The following day, we heard the sound of a motor lorry approaching and, peering through the cracks in the timbers of the barn, we saw spiked helmets and dived for the back of the pile of straw to burrow down close to the boards. After a while, we heard the barn door open and German voices and I caught the faint whiff of cigars. The Germans were moving the pile of straw but they were careless and didn't bother much beyond the front, and after a while the door creaked again and we heard the lorry moving away. Soon afterwards Marie-Ange called softly and as I pushed my head up I saw Sykes also emerging, ludicrously crowned with straw. Marie-

Ange's face creased with laughter, her eyes merry in a way I had never seen before.

'They go,' she said. 'They look for you but I do not think they expect to find you. They think you try to reach the Dutch frontier.' She paused, and her face became grave again. 'I have obtain hats for you,' she said. 'And old coats. Perhaps you must wear your uniforms underneath, otherwise they might shoot you as spies.'

'*I*'d make a fine spy,' I said. 'I can't even speak French.'

'We will go soon' – she paused – 'but first I think you will perhaps like to have the bath. I have make the fire hot and there is much water awaiting you.'

Sykes went first and I sat by the door of the barn with Marie-Ange, watching the road.

'It will be good to go back to England,' I said.

She sighed. 'I have often want to go back there,' she agreed. 'I much liked England. It is so much more grand and more beautiful than Belgium. What is it like where you live?'

'Flat,' I said. 'Like here. But nearer the sea. You can sail on the rivers and there are lots of birds.'

She looked at me solemnly. 'Perhaps soon you will see it again.'

'I hope so.'

'I have obtain thick socks and stout shoes for you. I think they will fit. I have write to my father.'

'You were taking a risk.'

'*Oui*,' she said calmly. '*C'est vrai*.'

'Do you realize what the penalties are?'

'*Oui. Certainement*.'

'It's dangerous.'

'So is to ride on a train, if one is not careful.'

I explained how the Germans had shot Nurse Cavell, the English nurse in Brussels whom they'd found helping British refugees to escape. She'd heard of her but she was unmoved.

'I wouldn't want that to happen,' I said and she gave a little laugh.

'Would you be sad if they shoot me?'

'Yes, I would.'

The laugh died and she looked at me with a quizzical expression. 'I do not believe you,' she said.

'It's true.'

'*Pourquoi?* Because I helped you?'

'Yes. That. And – well' – it was hard to explain and had something to do with being nineteen and with the way she managed to speak English – 'not just because of that,' I ended lamely.

She studied me for a long moment then she leaned forward and gave me a little peck on the cheek. I looked at her quickly and she explained. 'It does not mean anything,' she said. 'It is because I am eighteen now and I have not seen many young men except Germans.'

There was an awkward pause then she became brisk and business-like again.

'I do not say why I want the shoes,' she went on, 'but my father guesses, I think. They come to the post office this morning. I will bring them. I hope the sizes are right.'

'Mine are a bit on the big side,' I said. 'At school they used to say I was good at boxing because I was hard to knock down. There was so much of me along the floor.'

She laughed, her eyes lighting up.

'You look much prettier when you laugh,' I said in a strangled voice.

The smile died at once and she looked at me in a sort of mock gravity. 'I do not laugh much in the last three years,' she said.

'Perhaps I should make some funny faces,' I suggested.

I made one for her and she fell back in the straw, yelping with glee. When she sat up again, there was straw in her hair and she was still shaking.

'It is not the surprise that the Germans are frighten of the English fliers,' she said. 'Perhaps you make funny faces in the air at them.'

It was an idea that hadn't occurred to me, though there'd been a few times when my guns had jammed and it had been all I could do.

She was silent for a moment. 'I am sorry you will go,' she said after a while. 'There are no young people here for a long time.'

'You haven't a boy friend?'

She studied her feet, frowning a little as she did so. 'There is a boy. A long time ago. In Ghent. He is a neighbour. He go into the army. I do not see him since. I do not know whether he is alive now.'

'What was his name?'

She studied her feet a moment longer then she looked up and gave me a wide, mischievous smile. 'It is a long name. It will make you to laugh. It is Théophile Hyppolite Hyacinthe d'Ydewalle. He is a nice boy but that is all.'

I could see that with a name like that there might be difficulties.

'He'll come back after the war,' I said.

Her smile became sad. 'I think not,' she said, and I wondered if he'd been killed by the Germans.

She was silent for a while then she went on gravely.

'Monsieur le Major? Is he marry?'

'*Affiancé. Avec une de mes amis.*'

She stared at me. '*Et vous?* You have much girl friends?'

'No. None.'

'But surely they admire you? *Vous êtes très bien décoré.*' She touched the ribbons under my wings. 'I think much girls will be proud to be with you.'

'You'd be surprised,' I said. 'Mostly they behave as if I'd got the plague.'

She looked straight at me. '*I* would be proud,' she said.

–

In the next few days, I saw a lot of Marie-Ange as we made the final preparations for departure. The shoes she'd obtained for me were, inevitably, too small, but she took them back to the village and managed to exchange them with an elderly farm labourer she knew. Since they were new and of far better quality than the ugly old boots she got in exchange, I expect the farm labourer was only too willing.

'You now have the feet of an elephant,' Marie-Ange said.

'More like a large duck.'

She laughed. '*Que tu es drôle*,' she said.

I noticed she had suddenly started using the familiar 'tu' to me and I felt immensely pleased and flattered. But because I'd never expected in my life ever to be so friendly with any French-speaking foreigner I had never bothered to learn that part of the verb and I was in constant difficulties as I tried to respond on the same terms.

It only served to make her laugh more and I found I was enjoying making her laugh. It wasn't hard. I enjoyed being with her and was eager to see her smile and the way the lines appeared at the corner of her eyes. Her nose wrinkled when she laughed, too, and I spent a lot more of my time than I should have thinking up funny things to say to her.

We all knew the time for leaving was growing near, however, and finally she arrived through a thin drizzle of rain, her face solemn and with no sign of laughter.

'Tonight we must leave,' she said. 'Monsieur le Major, my mother has food which she wishes you will take.'

As Sykes vanished, Marie-Ange stared at me in that sobersides manner she had when she was troubled.

'I am sorry you must leave,' she said.

'So am I.'

'But it is necessary to win the war.'

'Yes, it is.' On my own, if necessary, I thought, so that the Germans would disappear and Marie-Ange could smile again.

'I will miss you.'

'I'll miss *you* Marie-Ange.'

'Perhaps one day you will return.'

'Not half.'

She seemed offended and I hurried to explain that 'not half' didn't mean a half-hearted interest in her but something considerably more. She seemed pleased and smiled again, but it was curiously grave.

'You have much funny words to say,' she said.

I put my hands to her elbows and managed to kiss her clumsily on the cheek. She didn't speak but stared at me with large grey eyes.

'This is not a true thing,' she said.

'Yes, it is, Marie-Ange.'

But she was wiser than I was. 'No. Perhaps when the Germans have gone and I see young Belgian boys in Ghent again I will not think so much about you. And perhaps when you are once more in England and you see the young English girls you also will feel different.'

I had to admit that it was possibly true, but I promised I'd never forget her and we exchanged addresses, then I stamped the two great boots I was wearing.

'Like a duck,' I said, and she laughed and flung her arms round me and hugged me.

–

We set off from Noyelles soon after dark and, since the autumn had now arrived, it wasn't late. Marie-Ange appeared at the entrance to the barn wearing a cloak with a hood, and stout boots and thick stockings. They gave her a lost-little-girl look, with the drizzle on her hair and eyelashes. Her parting from her mother seemed particularly emotional and the old lady's eyes were streaming. Sykes was grave and silent and made kissing Madame's hand seem twice as important, then we were tramping through the rain in the increasing darkness.

Marie-Ange knew her way all right. 'I have walk before to Middelkerke,' she said. 'One time we walk to Ghent to see my father.'

We didn't speak much and tramped through the puddles silently, aware of the drizzle soaking our clothes. Marie-Ange seemed to be made of fine springs and never seemed to be tired and I decided that working on a farm was better practice for this sort of thing than sitting in an aeroplane. I was tired long before she was.

We halted to eat bread and meat from the haversack Sykes carried, sitting in the shadows at the side of the road under a clump of trees. As it was growing daylight, Marie-Ange pointed to a timbered barn in a field. 'We will rest the day there,' she said. 'I have write them a letter. They know we will be there, but they are not interest to seeing us. They have much fear.'

The barn was dry and comfortable and there was plenty of fresh straw. And placed prominently on an old crate was a bottle of rough wine, a loaf and cheese.

Marie-Ange smiled delightedly. 'Someone has leave their supper,' she said.

We were all hungry after the night's march in the cool air and drizzle and we tore the loaf apart and shared the cheese and wine. When we'd finished, we dug into the straw. It was warm under there and I was half-asleep before I was even comfortable.

It must have been late in the afternoon when I awoke. Marie-Ange's head was on my shoulder but she started to wakefulness immediately when I moved.

'Soon is it time to walk again,' she said.

The drizzle had stopped but there was a lot of cloud and it seemed chilly with the damp of the low-lying fields. The farm seemed deserted but somewhere not far away I could hear a woman's voice and the sound of wood being sawn.

No one came near us, however, and we slipped away in the dusk and began to head north again. Sykes was walking well but I found the big boots Marie-Ange had found for me were heavy and beginning to rub my heel.

'You are limping,' Marie-Ange said.

'It's having such big feet,' Sykes said mercilessly. 'More to rub.'

That night was much colder than the previous one and the wind was blowing from the west again bringing with it the thud of guns and a hint of more rain. We still had about sixty kilometres to go and I was already tired.

Through my mind a whole host of thoughts were running. I was making up a brave little farewell speech for when we had to leave Marie-Ange behind. I wasn't looking forward to it but I felt I had to put on some sort of show to make her realize how grateful we were and how pleased I was that I'd met her. It all seemed a little inadequate, however, and as I tried to improve on it the speech grew in my mind into an oration in which I made it clear how brave I thought her, how intelligent, how beautiful, and how delightful when she laughed, and I wondered if I ought to accompany it with a chaste kiss. Sykes, I thought, might even have the grace to turn his back for a while so that I could put my arms round her and make a proper job of it for a change.

She seemed to sense something was troubling me and after a while, she touched my hand as though to encourage me and we walked hand-in-hand in the darkness. But walking hand-in-hand belongs to warm evenings and strolling across fields, not slogging heavily in the damp night air, and we soon reverted to the steady trudge, one foot after the other, left, right, left, right, left, right.

I was walking head down, indifferent to the flickering western horizon and not really thinking about anything, when Sykes, who was just in front, stopped so suddenly I crashed into his back. I scraped my nose on the buckle of the haversack he was carrying and cursed him.

'Shut up,' he said sharply.

'What is it?' Marie-Ange demanded.

'Look,' Sykes said, jerking a hand.

It was only just possible to make him out and when I looked through the darkness to where he was pointing all I could see was what looked like the end of a large building among the trees.

'It's only a barn,' I said.

'Is it?' Sykes said. 'Look to the left a bit.'

We were in a small depression at the time, where the road ran between higher ground on either side. My eye moved to the left and I saw a pair of parallel lines against the sky – and V-shaped struts between them. And then a shark-like nose and a propeller.

'Aeroplanes,' I breathed.

'German aeroplanes,' Sykes agreed.

Marie-Ange looked agitated. 'We must not to stay here,' she said. 'There will be guards.'

Sykes took her arm and pulled her into the shadow of some low shrubs. 'Where are we?' he demanded.

'This is Phalempon. The village is over there.'

Sykes drew a deep breath. 'Marie-Ange,' he said. 'This is as far as we go.'

She looked puzzled. '*Je ne comprends pas.*'

'I have a better idea than going by boat. Let's *fly* back.'

'In an aeroplane?' I said.

'I hadn't thought of feathers.' Sykes jerked a hand and we moved forward to the rising ground, and crept slowly up it. Lying flat in the damp grass at the top, we could see a wide space and more aeroplanes which had been invisible from the lower ground. What I had thought was a barn was a canvas hangar.

'Albatros DIIIs or DVs,' Sykes said. 'Couldn't we fly 'em?'

'No!' Marie-Ange's reaction was vehement. 'This is not good!'

For once I didn't agree with her. What Sykes was suggesting made sense. 'Marie-Ange,' I said. 'Instead of taking all night to sneak past the German patrol boats, it'll take only half an hour.'

'See any guards?' Sykes asked.

In the distance across the field I could see lights but no movement. 'I'll bet they're there all right,' I said. 'They told me when they caught me it'd be no good trying to grab an aeroplane.'

'*One* of us might,' Sykes said. 'If we start something at opposite ends of the line.'

We spent the next few minutes arguing fiercely over the merits and demerits of Sykes' idea. Marie-Ange obviously didn't like it. She knew nothing about aeroplanes and she gripped my hand fiercely as we talked in low voices.

'You will be shot!'

Neither of us was listening to her now, though. Our minds were racing with the possibility of what lay in front of us.

'We couldn't fly an aeroplane off on a pitch-black night,' I said.

Sykes gestured. 'We've flown in the dark,' he said. 'Both of us.'

'We'd be better leaving at first light.'

Suddenly the plan seemed foolhardy, but Sykes prevailed and we agreed to scout round the field. Marie-Ange was unhappy about the whole thing. Her mind seemed full of foreboding and she was anxious to get away before we were found. But Sykes had got the idea firmly fixed in his head now and we decided to move round the perimeter away from where the lights lay.

'It's hopeless,' I said after a while. 'The machines are all too close to the huts. We'd be safer in a boat.'

Marie-Ange looked hopeful but Sykes pulled a face. 'Always seasick,' he said. 'Rotten sailor.'

I didn't believe him because I knew he had his mind set on doing the job by air. But it seemed impossible to steal an aeroplane from in front of the hangars and after a lot of arguing we decided to spend the rest of the night among the bushes at the end of the field farthest from the huts and hangars and watch what happened the following day. Marie-Ange fought fiercely against it. 'No,' she said. 'It is bad. It is much dangerous.'

I thought so, too, but we found a spot in the bushes to hole up in and crouched together in a huddle. Against the growing morning light, Sykes' face had a bleak eager look.

It was cold and I found I kept breaking into uncontrollable shivers, but I knew it was nothing to do with the night air. Marie-Ange seemed suddenly calm, however, as though she had decided to argue no longer.

As we waited for morning, we could hear the guns muttering away to the west and see the flickering lights against the horizon that indicated the front line. After a while I noticed that the sky behind us was growing paler.

'Fun'll start soon,' Sykes said. 'The early morning boys'll be off and we'll be able to see what happens.'

More lights were appearing now by the hangars, one of them bobbing among the line of aeroplanes. A square of yellow appeared, as though someone had opened a door.

'Gone for their hard-boiled eggs,' Sykes said.

He seemed altogether too flippant about the whole thing but I knew it didn't mean anything. He was probably as nervous as I was and was trying to hide the fact. Then suddenly, the silence was split by the roar of an aeroplane engine starting up.

'We're off,' Sykes said. 'Warming up for the early patrol.'

Marie-Ange was crouching silently beside me and, glancing at her in the growing light, I saw there were tears on her cheeks.

'Why, Marie-Ange?' I asked. 'Why?'

She shrugged, in a peculiarly Gallic gesture. 'Because you are much brave and silly,' she said.

Another engine started up. 'Expect it's the same at Bayeffles,' Sykes said.

'I wish I were back there,' I commented without thinking, and saw Marie-Ange look quickly at me.

Another engine started and I could see the field taking shape now and the dark blocks of the huts and a thin streamer of smoke rising into the sky.

'Any minute now it'll be daylight,' Sykes said.

I had been silent and listening and I gave him a jab. 'Dry up,' I said. 'Listen!'

He cocked his head and caught the sound I'd heard – the faint hum of aeroplane engines.

'Somebody up early,' he said.

'Yes. And what's more, they're coming this way.'

Automatically, I put my arm round Marie-Ange's shoulders and pushed her closer to the ground. There was a long pause. The low hum was still audible but across the field where the hangars were it had clearly not yet been heard above the clatter of the morning duties, the clink of spanners and the noise of metal panels being removed, and the squeak of carts carrying ammunition belts.

A dog barked and I felt so tense I thought I was going to choke.

The hum of aeroplane engines was growing louder now and suddenly the men at the other end of the field woke up to it, too. There were staccato shouts and I saw them starting to run. Almost at once we heard the snarl of engines approaching from beyond the trees at tremendous speed and the sudden clack-clack of machine guns.

I grabbed Marie-Ange and thrust her down into the bushes.

'For God's sake,' Sykes was saying furiously. 'It's the Navy!'

Four black triplanes were coming over the trees at the far end of the field and I saw the earth erupt near the huts as bombs fell, then a second later the triplanes were howling past our heads.

'The swine!' Sykes roared furiously, pounding at the top of the bank with his fist. 'They've done it across us! They'll double the guards now and we'll never pinch anything.'

The triplanes were turning in a steep bank now a quarter of a mile away for a second run across the field. One of the huts at the far end was blazing and in the growing daylight I could see men running. Then I saw that one of the Albatroses had got away and was moving towards us down the field to get into position for a take-off into wind. It was a grey-and-green machine with a large letter K on the fuselage just behind the Maltese Crosses.

'Damn them!' Sykes said furiously, staring at the sky. 'They've got the sea! What more do they want?'

The grey-and-green Albatros was still moving towards us, its wings rocking as its wheels rolled over the uneven surface of the field. Several more were following it but the triplanes were coming down again now. I saw a hut go up in a shower of planks and debris, then three of the moving machines were hit, one after the other. A bomb dropped alongside one of them and it flipped neatly over on its back and burst into flames. The pilot scrambled clear and began to run from the path of the other two, but another triplane screamed down, its guns rattling, and I saw him go head over heels like a shot rabbit and one of the following Albatroses bumped over his body and then that one was hit, too, and burst into flames. The pilot of the third machine also seemed to have been hit because he was careering about the field in an indeterminate way, and he finally crashed into the machine which had flipped over on to its back. I heard the crunch as he ploughed into the starboard wings, even above the crack of the bombs and the clatter of machine guns and the shouts across the field.

The triplanes had gone now, as suddenly as they'd come, and the grey-and-green Albatros was near the end of the field immediately in front of us, swinging round to take off after them, its propeller idling, as though the pilot were trying to make up his mind which way to go to avoid the debris scattered across the centre of the landing area. Suddenly I realized Sykes was struggling out of the haversack and thrusting it at Marie-Ange. Then he wrenched off the old coat she'd acquired for him and threw it down.

'Now,' he screamed. 'Now!'

I knew at once what he intended and I swung round and kissed the startled Marie-Ange full on the lips. 'Run!' I yelled. 'Get away from here as fast as you can!'

We didn't even have a chance to say good-bye because she was already thrusting through the bushes away from the airfield while I was wrenching off the coat I was wearing and scrambling with Sykes over the lip of the rise to where the Albatros waited.

Chapter 10

It stuck out a mile that there was a chance for one of us to escape right there in front of us, because there seemed to be complete confusion at the far end of the field. One of the hangars and two of the huts were blazing and, as I scrambled over the rise, I could see the gap where a bomb had removed another hut. The aeroplanes there were all mixed up together, facing in every possible direction, as though in their haste to get clear they had simply got in each other's way, and mechanics were frantically dragging at them to swing them round so they could head for the take-off area.

The grey-and-green Albatros was turning now to head diagonally across the field. I heard the engine roar and thought we were too late, but then I saw Sykes jump on the wing, and, throwing an arm round the German pilot's neck, reach past him into the cockpit. The engine blared but even as the machine moved forward it died again and the aeroplane slowed to a stop, its tail swinging wildly.

'For God's sake,' Sykes yelled. 'Hurry, Brat!'

I had grabbed a piece of stone from the bank as I had jumped over its lip and the next moment I was plunging through the slipstream as the engine died and on to the other wing. The German was fighting furiously under Sykes' grip, and was still threshing away with his free arm when I hit him over the head with the stone.

He immediately slumped in the cockpit. 'I've killed him,' I said.

'Shouldn't think so,' Sykes panted. 'But he's going to have a headache. Get him out, for God's sake!'

The German was a big man and neither Sykes nor I were, and it was harder than I'd ever imagined. I'd helped lift injured men from cockpits before but there'd always been plenty of assistance and plenty of time, and this time there was neither and he seemed to have his legs jammed somewhere inside. Sykes was panting and cursing in a way I'd never heard before as we fought to drag him free.

'How are we going to do it?' I shouted in a panic of excitement and fright. 'One of us riding on the wing? We'll never get away with it.'

'No – oh, for God's sake, this damn' man! – two in the cockpit! You on my knees! I've got longer legs!'

'Two in the cockpit!' I tried to reach past the German to free him. 'Can't be done.'

'It's a big cockpit.' Sykes' voice came in a panting rush. 'Albatroses are. It's not a Pup and neither of us is a giant. Do it like we learned to fly. In the old Longhorns.'

I knew at once what he had in mind. In the Farman Longhorn, the instructor had sat in front, while the pupil sat behind, his legs on either side feeling the extra rudder bar, his arms holding on to extensions to the controls. I knew at once it would work if we could only get the German free.

Inevitably the struggle had been noticed by this time and I could see men running across the field, and then a car burst out of the confusion round the hangars, its engine howling. A shot was fired and I heard the bullet 'whack' past and whine away into the distance.

We nearly had the German free by this time, but he seemed to be bent backwards like a bow and his feet were now under the dashboard somehow and he was beginning to come round and struggle feebly.

Sykes yelled as he came free at last, and I fell in a heap on the grass with him. For a second I thought we'd lose the aeroplane because the propeller was still turning but Sykes was still on the wing and was scrambling now into the cockpit.

'For God's sake,' he screamed, and I ran after him as he swung the machine into wind. Hardly looking where I put my feet I scrambled up the round belly and flopped into the cockpit on to his knees. It was a tremendous jam and there didn't seem any room to move the joystick.

'Let her rip,' he yelled and I opened the throttle immediately without really thinking of the consequences.

Sykes couldn't see a thing except round my body, but his long legs were on either side of me on the rudder bar, while I held the joystick and the throttle. As we bumped across the grass, I stared at the dials and indicators, and the *Johannisthal* plate on the dashboard that indicated the plane's origin.

'What's "Zu" stand for?' I yelled. 'And "Haup-tank"?'

Fortunately, I was able to assume that the engine was warm and primed, and all I needed to do was hold the stick back as the speed built up. The German pilot was on his feet now and was dragging at a revolver. As we swung round I heard it go off and my right leg leapt.

'Oh, God,' I yelped, in a panic of fright. 'He's hit me!'

'Bad?' Sykes yelled back.

I felt sure it was but I didn't seem to be dying and I was far more concerned with the fact that at that moment we were facing directly towards the burning aeroplane. 'Rudder!' I screamed. 'Right rudder! She's swinging!'

Sykes' legs moved.

'Not too much! That'll do!'

As the speed built up the aeroplane swung wildly then hurtled forward. I couldn't read the airspeed indicator because it was set out in kilometres but I had been at the game long enough to fly by the seat of my trousers and could tell by the feel when she was ready to lift off.

The Germans were still running towards us and the car was moving in front of us now. I saw a mechanic grab for the wing but we were moving too fast by this time and I saw him go head over heels as it sent him flying. Then I pushed the stick forward and the tail came up. The car swung across our path and it looked as though there was going to be the most almighty crash. I yanked frantically on the stick although I sensed we hadn't yet built up flying speed, and the nose lifted and the wheels came off the ground. But we weren't moving fast enough and they touched again and we bounced, but I was still heaving at the stick and at last the nose lifted. I saw men jumping out of the car and a German officer standing in the back seat firing at us with a pistol. Where the bullets went I had no idea, but I heard a 'whangg' as one of them hit the cowling, then he took a dive over the side as the Albatros lifted over him.

I caught a whiff of burning oil as we flashed through the drifting smoke from the blazing aeroplanes, then we were roaring over the huts towards the trees. I saw men with rifles firing and a machine gun on a cartwheel swinging round. A little flag of fabric began to flap on the lower wing and the trees seemed to be rushing towards us, growing enormously in size until they seemed to fill the whole of my view. I headed for the smallest.

'The trees!' Sykes screamed, his mouth by my ear. 'The trees! Lift her!'

'She won't come up,' I screamed back. 'She's too heavy!'

With two aboard, the Albatros was taking a long time to climb and I saw the trees flash past on either side. For a moment I thought we'd gone through them.

'Think we clipped 'em,' Sykes yelled. 'Saw a lot of flying leaves.'

We were clear of the airfield at last and I found the rising sun and swung in a wide circle to put it behind me on course for the west. Sykes was staring backwards and downwards, looking for Germans, but my eye was searching the roads. After a while I caught sight of a small figure that I knew instinctively was Marie-Ange's. She'd not wasted time and had already put a good distance between herself and the aerodrome and I felt thankful for that. Then I saw her lift her arm and the frantic flutter of a white handkerchief as she slipped backwards, a small forlorn figure, out of sight below the wing. I realized then that I hadn't said a single one of the things I'd wanted to say to her. Nothing else but 'Run! Get away from here as fast as you can!' It hardly seemed to express what I'd wanted to say. And that chaste kiss I'd decided on had turned out to be nothing more than a hurried peck as I'd scrambled for the bank.

It was a good job Sykes was with me because he didn't give me the chance to think about it long.

'A couple of 'em are off,' he yelled in my ear. 'They're coming after us.'

Sitting on his knee I was half out of the cockpit and, with the wind flattening my hair, half-frozen in the slipstream. The Albatros felt as though she'd been crash-landed at some point in her career and they'd never been able to true the rigging up and she seemed to fly left-wing-low, while the Mercedes engine was throwing out oil which I could feel spattering my face in a fine mist mixed with odd larger globules.

'How's the leg?' Sykes yelled.

I'd almost forgotten it but now I realized it was painful and felt sure I could feel the blood running in bucketfuls into my boot. 'Numb,' I shouted.

'Better turn the wick up a bit,' Sykes suggested. 'Those two behind are catching up.'

I juggled with the throttle but it didn't seem to make much difference.

'Won't go any faster,' I said. 'Carrying too much weight.'

'Coming up fast,' Sykes yelled and, turning my head, I saw the two Germans right behind us, climbing for height. I decided there was no point in trying to get up very high. We had only a matter of ten miles to go but I knew they were going to be the longest ten miles I'd ever flown.

'Better cock the guns,' Sykes advised. 'Might need 'em.'

It seemed a good idea.

With its extra load, the Albatros was sluggish and there was nothing I could do about it. We were only about a hundred feet up, just skimming the tops of the tall poplars, and I saw a ruined church spire flash past, all the slates missing and the laths showing. Faces were staring up at us, white against the brown earth, and I saw horses and guns moving forward to the lines, their drivers also gazing up, obviously wondering why two German aeroplanes were advancing with such menace on a third.

'Here they come,' Sykes shouted. 'For what we are about to receive may the Lord make us truly thankful!'

I heard the clatter behind and there was a whack of bullets passing through the wings and I saw the tracer trails and smelt the smoke of the bullets.

'Port,' Sykes yelled and, as he kicked at the rudder bar, I shoved the stick over and we skidded away from them.

There was another sharp ack–ack–ack behind us and I knew by the sound that the German was dangerously close by now.

'Port again!' Sykes roared and we skidded away again.

'We can't keep going to port,' I screamed. 'We'll end up back at Phalempon.'

'Have it your own way, but the Huns are to starboard!'

The rattle of guns sounded again and splinters leapt from the edge of the wing. We skidded away again, to starboard this time as the German flashed past, and for a moment I thought we were going to hit the second German who came up unexpectedly on that side. By the grace of God, he pulled away in time, and as the first one banked steeply to come behind us again, I saw we'd been given a minute or two of grace before he got into position once more, and pushed the nose down to gain speed.

I could see the lines now just in front and a whole string of shell-bursts. The thought that we were going to be flying through the barrage just as the shells reached the last few yards of their downward arc made my stomach turn over but there was no chance to do anything about it. The Germans were coming up behind us again and they must have been so furious or so excited at seeing us escaping they, too, didn't bother to turn aside. I heard the machine guns go again and saw more flags of fabric flap. A bullet whanged against the engine cover somewhere and I heard it scream away. A large hole appeared above my head and more splinters flew.

Between us we managed to fling the machine away from the stream of bullets but, sitting high out of the cockpit without a safety belt, I seemed to flop about like a jelly on a hot plate. My leg seemed to be stiffening, too, and I was certain now that my boot was full of blood.

'Gettin' warm,' Sykes roared. 'Can't you do anythin' about it?'

'No!'

'Thought you were a dab hand with an aeroplane?'

'If you think you can do any better,' I yelled back, 'we'll change places.'

The Germans seemed to be sitting just behind us now, potting at us every few seconds, and why neither of us was hit I couldn't imagine because the Albatros seemed to be falling to pieces about our ears. But I could see barbed wire now. It was new wire and hadn't gone rusty, and it lay over the ground like a pale blue mist. Then Sykes started hammering at my back and, turning my head, I saw him pointing. Though I couldn't get round properly, I saw the flat top wings and the dihedral of the lower wings that stamped a group of Camels coming down.

The Albatroses had seen them, too, because one of them was swinging away to bolt for home. The second seemed to decide on one last try and came in again for us. I felt sure this time that the Albatros was going to fall apart but it kept on flying even when I threw it in as tight a bank as I dared. As we came round we were face to face with the German who was going round in the opposite direction and I pressed the trigger of the guns. I smelled cordite and saw the guns jumping and he began to wobble and I saw a puff of smoke, then he had flashed past and I was too busy simply keeping the machine flying to worry about what had happened to him.

'He's gone,' Sykes roared. 'And the Camels have got the other! We're all right now… Oh, my God!' – his voice rose to a scream – '*No, no!*'

I didn't have to look to guess what had happened. The Camels hadn't noticed what was going on and had seen only three German Albatroses apparently larking about close to the ground. They had disposed of one and probably we had disposed of the other and now they were coming down on us.

The Mercedes engine was making weird noises now, as though something were loose inside, and I had an awful sensation that the wings were about to fall off. But we were over the German front line now and crossing the blue belt of barbed wire.

The first Camel came in so close I could see the oil on the engine cowling catching the early morning sun. The guns rattled and the Albatros took more punishment, but by the grace of God once again we weren't hit ourselves. The engine was labouring badly now, though, and I could see smoke coming in puffs from it and could even smell it.

'We're on fire!'

'Keep it up,' Sykes roared. 'Only a bit further!'

But the Albatros was barely flying now. I could see wires trailing and hear them twanging all round us and I knew that if I tried to dodge the next Camel that came down the wings would simply fall off. But the Camels seemed to consider that they had done all that was necessary and, probably hoping we'd land intact, they were waiting just above for us to crash. I didn't think they'd have to wait long.

I saw the shell-holes come up in front then another belt of wire and the British trenches.

'We've made it,' I yelled, then to my horror a positive fusillade came up at us. Both sides were shooting at us now. The Germans had long since spotted two heads and caught on that something was wrong and had opened up with rifles and machine guns, while the British, seeing only black crosses on the wings, were doing the same. The wings looked like sieves by this time and the engine gave one last despairing clang and stopped. The propeller jerked twice and halted in a horizontal position, and in the silence all I could hear was the hum of the wind through what wires still remained and the roar of battle about me.

I had never realized just what a lot of noise went on in the front line. I could hear machine guns rattling away steadily in short bursts and the separate pop of rifles, the whole lot backgrounded by the thump and crash of shells.

We floated over the British front line, barely flying, and I saw a shell explode just in front, then we were drifting through the smoke and the clods of earth and the spray of water it had thrown up. The ground was only just beneath us now, and there was a ruined cottage just ahead right in our path. I tried to bank to starboard but I knew I couldn't and the wingtip caught the gable end. I felt the aeroplane lurch and pieces of wood and metal fell off, then the wheels touched and the machine, still miraculously upright, rolled along what must have been the only piece of flat dry land for miles around and dropped neatly into a shell-hole. The tail came up, and I was surrounded by a violent crunching, crashing sound, then everything went black.

I came round with a pain in my face and firmly convinced I was dead. Foul-tasting water was in my mouth and eyes and nose. I tried to raise my head but a tremendous weight came down on it, shoving my face into the water again. With the desperation of the drowning, I fought free and found I was sprawling at the bottom of the shell-hole with Sykes alongside me. He had fallen out of the cockpit straight on top of me and seemed to have fared better than I had. My nose was bleeding where I'd banged it in the crash and I felt sure I was dying. Sykes didn't waste time sympathizing, however. He grabbed me by the collar and as he dragged me free from the aeroplane I realized that, just to make things complete, I was saturated with petrol.

A shell exploded just over the lip of the crater, showering us with earth and stones and water and we scrabbled in the torn surface trying to bury ourselves in the soil. I was frightened to death and almost weeping with fury that this should happen to us after all we'd been through. The water in the bottom of the shell-hole was foul and green and stank abominably, then it suddenly dawned on us that we'd made it, and, sprawling in the slime in the bottom of the shell-hole, we leapt at each other delightedly.

My leg gave way as I jumped up and I fell help-lessly against Sykes, clawing at him for support. But it didn't matter that my breeches were soaked with blood. I knew no bones were broken and we were delirious with joy, pounding each other's shoulders, our faces streaked with dirt, our hair flattened by the wind and drenched by the water, rolling and yelling and laughing, until we must have looked like a couple of drunken puppies wallowing about, both of us covered with mud and the blood from my nose.

'Beat the whole bloomin' German air force,' Sykes shouted.

'And the whole bloomin' British air force!'

'*And* the German army!'

'And the British army!'

'Navy, too, come to that!'

We leapt at each other again, but this time, the antics were brought up short by a dry rasping voice that sounded like Munro's.

'Hands up, ye Prussian bastards, or Ah'll gi'e ye four inches o' cold steel richt doon the throat.'

It brought us up sharp and we released each other to turn round and stare open-mouthed at a soldier in a mud-caked helmet peering at us over the lip of the shell-hole. He was a sergeant and alongside him two other men appeared. They were all three heavily moustached, their faces black with dirt, their uniforms and kilts covered with mud.

Sykes grinned. 'We're English,' he said. 'English pilots. We've just escaped.'

'Aye, tell me anither yin.'

Sykes looked up indignantly. 'We're wearing British uniforms, aren't we, man?' he said.

'Could ye no' be spies?'

'We *are* British!' I scrambled to my knees and screeched at him in fury, terrified he'd shoot me after the effort we'd made to escape. 'We pinched the damn' thing and flew it back!'

'Hoo do *Ah* ken ye're British?'

Sykes looked up, gave him a brilliant beaming smile and began to swear. He used all the good old Anglo-Saxon words he had ever heard uttered by sullen privates in a cavalry stables, together with all those he'd gathered from raw-knuckled fitters crouched over recalcitrant engines on frozen mornings, and rounded them off with a few he'd doubtless picked up in the hunting field and from poachers round Hathersett village. I stared admiringly. So did the sergeant.

His moustache lifted and they all three of them began to grin. The rifles they were pointing at us dropped.

'Och, aye,' the sergeant said. 'Ah ken fine ye're British.'

They jumped into the shell-hole and offered cigarettes.

'For God's sake,' Sykes said. 'Don't light up, or we'll go up in flames! We're drenched in petrol.'

They dragged me out of the shell-hole belly-down to the ground while machine gun bullets whack-whacked over the top of us, uncomfortably close. A shell burst and they ducked, then the sergeant lifted his head.

'Now,' he yelled. 'Run!'

He jumped to his feet with the others and they dragged me with them, heads down, until we fell into a trench, all in a heap on top of each other.

The sergeant heaved me to my feet and sat me on the firestep. 'Ah reckon the C.O.'ll want to see ye, laddie,' he said paternally. 'Ye'd better come this way. He's frae Edinburgh an' he keeps a gey fine dram o' whisky.'

The sergeant's commanding officer gave us all a drink and telephoned to Wing for us, then they bandaged my leg – which turned out to be not half as bad as I'd expected – and sent us down the line with an escort to help me along. When we got back to the aerodrome, it was like a riot – especially with Sykes turning up, too – and Munro and Bull were capering round us as if they were mad.

'And what's more, mon,' Munro yelled in a frenzy of delight. 'We're gettin' Camels! It's official!'

It was wonderful to be back and send the telegrams home but right at the height of the party that Munro insisted on starting, I went outside, leaning heavily on a stick someone had given me. The horizon was still flickering with the shell fire and I could hear the thud of explosions and the faint rattle of machine guns. Suddenly I found Sykes alongside me. 'Lookin' for the dawn risin', Brat, old son?' he asked gently.

I nodded, but I wasn't really. I was remembering Marie-Ange and her lonely walk home, because it had suddenly occurred to me that perhaps the reason she'd been so eager for us to go by boat was because she'd decided to come, too. I had remembered the tears in her mother's eyes and had suddenly wondered if she'd been saying good-bye. She'd often said she wanted to see England again, and if that had been in her mind, her return to the farm would be twice as wretched.

'Penny for 'em, Brat,' Sykes said.

I could hear the noise in the mess and Munro shouting out a song at the piano.

'It's the only, only way,
It's the only trick to play—'

'Not worth a penny,' I said.

'You realize they'll send us home, don't you?' he said. 'Policy for escapers. In case we're shot down and captured again. Could be awkward. 'Sides, you're wounded. Intrepid birdman hurt in a death dive.'

I grinned. 'How long will it be for?' I asked.

He shrugged. 'Just till the Germans have forgotten us, I suppose.'

I nodded. It made sense. But I had one thing to do first, leg or no leg. Sykes was going to find himself organizing a patrol towards Noyelles. He didn't know it yet, but he was, and I was going to be on it. And there was going to be a message dropped near that great Dutch barn where we'd spent so long hiding in the straw. I was already looking forward to seeing that small solemn figure by the house and the sudden frantic waving I knew would follow when she guessed who it was.